# HIS GUNS BLAZED . . . AND MEN DIED

They called him Six-Gun "Melody" Madigan for two good reasons. The first was his talent for loud but tuneless singing. The second and most deadly reason was his virtuosity with a .45 Colt. His six-guns played a tune that struck terror into the hearts of the cattle rustlers and swindlers in the Du Sang mob.

And the sleepy town of Vaca Wells would hear plenty of hair-trigger music before Melody was through!

# SIX-GUN
# MELODY

## William Colt
## Macdonald

**AVON**
PUBLISHERS OF BARD, CAMELOT, DISCUS, EQUINOX AND FLARE BOOKS

AVON BOOKS
A division of
The Hearst Corporation
959 Eighth Avenue
New York, New York 10019

ISBN: 0-380-00068-7

First Avon Printing, January, 1953
Third Printing

AVON TRADEMARK REG. U.S. PAT. OFF. AND
FOREIGN COUNTRIES, REGISTERED TRADEMARK—
MARCA REGISTRADA, HECHO EN CHICAGO, U.S.A.

Printed in the U.S.A.

# Principal Characters

### "MELODY" MADIGAN
Tall, redheaded cowpuncher. Fast on the draw and one of the best shots in cow country—as the local bad men learn to their sorrow.

### BULL BADGLEY
Surly, tough, and expert with a gun. Not averse to shooting an unarmed opponent. Slick at altering cattle brands.

### THE DU SANG BROTHERS
Hugo, Luke, and Guy Du Sang, owners of the Diamond-8 Ranch. They are anxious to increase their herds and land-holdings—and don't believe in buying either!

### MANITOBA
Professional killer hired by Diamond-8 to "go to work" on Melody.

### TOM NORRIS
Weathered, old-time rancher; owner of Rafter-S Ranch; father of "Jerry."

### "JERRY" NORRIS
Pretty, copper-haired daughter of Tom Norris. Her unquenchable spirit helps her father to hang on to his ranch, even though his cattle are disappearing faster than they normally increase—and *not* because of *four-legged* wolves!

# PART I

## *Trouble Breaks*

## *1.*

MAYBE it was too much cheap whisky that brought about the trouble between Melody Madigan and Bull Badgely. Perhaps the bad weather had something to do with it. It may have been a combination of both. From the very beginning, beef roundup on the Crossed-Anchors range had, it seemed, been hoodooed. One man had been gored by a steer; another had lost two fingers when his hand became caught between the saddle horn and a taut rope; the horse of a third had gone over a cut bank, breaking its leg and putting its rider out of commission for several weeks to come.

It was one of those nasty autumns. Gray skies. Rain. Snow. Sleet overhead and slush underfoot. Disagreeable working under such conditions, and it was commencing to tell on the men's nerves. Montana falls are like that, sometimes. Being short-handed didn't improve affairs, either. But there was no help for it. The Old Man was driving the boys at a terrific rate, doing his best to force things to a finish before the weather became any worse.

Normally even tempers commenced to display raw edges. Growls were heard more often than jokes. It kept the Old Man busy breaking up fights, and he always heaved a long sigh of relief when breakfast was concluded and the hands had loped off to the day's work. He knew that by the time night fell, they would be feeling too miserable to do much more than eat supper and crawl, shivering and soaked to the skin, into their blankets.

Of all the crew, Bull Badgely "crabbed" loudest, Melody Madigan had the least grumbling to do. But after all, Melody always had been a cheerful sort of cuss regardless of conditions. Badgely had arranged with friends in town to bring him liquor every so often, and he managed to keep his skin well-soaked. He carried a well-filled flask at all times, and stiff drinks of fiery "red-eye" comprised his earliest breakfast and latest supper. Not that Badgely ever got real drunk; he just consumed enough to make him mean.

He was a big, hulking brute of a man with coarse black hair, a flattened nose, and a pugnacious, unshaven jaw. A good puncher, when he worked—which wasn't often—and a fast man with a six-gun.

Melody Madigan was a tall, lean-limbed and sinewy-jawed cowboy with flaming red hair, humorous gray eyes, and the whitest teeth in the world. No one knew who had tacked the name "Melody" on him, but it probably had something to do with the battered old accordion he carried back of his saddle. One old-timer had explained Melody Madigan as "the man who put the harmony in Colt music." Be that as it may, there's no dodging the fact that Madigan could shoot as well with his right hand as he could with his left, and both hands worked far better than average.

Bull Badgely resented this. Up until the time Melody joined the Crossed-Anchors outfit, Bull's record as a marksman had gone unchallenged. However, a certain Fourth of July contest had elevated Melody to a higher place. As time passed, Madigan proved his supremacy in other lines, too—riding, roping, and everyday cow knowledge. The deep hate of jealousy commenced to corrode Badgely's disposition, and he longed for an opportunity to regain his lost laurels. And yet he didn't quite dare foment an open break. The time hadn't come for that.

One dismal morning, however, towards the close of the roundup, the cook's "C'mon an' get it, or I'll throw it on the ground," roused the outfit to the fact that another day was about to dawn. A wet drizzle was falling, half snow, half rain, and freezing almost as soon as it touched the earth. The wind was blowing a gale, knife-edged like a blast from the Arctic. It wasn't yet daylight, and the early morning chill penetrated to the marrow.

Melody moved reluctantly under ice-stiffened blankets, as the cook enforced his words with resounding bangs on the dish-pan. Down near the remuda the horse wrangler was cursing in a loud voice about something or other that had gone wrong. All around Melody, lumped shapes were yawning and stretching, swearing and grumbling. The

8

flickering lights escaping from cookie's fire shone coldly on the slanting arrows of rain.

The Old Man was up, now. "Rouse out, you butterflies," he bawled, "an' crawl outta your cocoons!"

Melody sat up, settled his sombrero on his head. "Too much noise to sleep longer, anyhow," he grunted good-naturedly. He reached for his boots, which were stiff with cold, and thrust his feet into their icy depths. Then with numbed fingers he commenced to roll a cigarette, the wind and rain beating into his chilled features.

The smoke was warming to his lungs. He sat there a few moments, gazing around the camp. Some short distance away the light from the fire picked out highlights on a tilted bottle in the hands of Bull Badgely. Melody caught the sound of an oath as Badgely put down the bottle. Bull had been refusing a drink to one of the other men.

"Nice generous cuss, that Badgely," Melody said to himself. "Howsomever, he's welcome to that stuff he drinks." The cowboy got to his feet, stamped the cigarette butt under his toe and nearly slipped in the wet mud.

He was first to answer the call for breakfast. The others stumbled up, dragging weary feet and voicing grumbling words against the weather, the cook, the outfit, and anything else that happened to strike their fancy.

"Damn! More rain!" one of them growled.

Melody, standing at the other side of the fire with a cup of steaming coffee in his hand, chuckled. "Rain, rain, the beautiful rain," he quoted softly. "Shucks! Billings, you shouldn't mind the rain. God sends the rain to make the pretty things grow. Mebbe it'll help you some."

Billings shivered, and glared at Melody without answering. The other men gathered around to the accompanying clatter of tin plates, smacking of lips and some conversation. Mostly, though, attention was concentrated on the consuming of hot Java. The Old Man talked about the day's work, but no one paid any great attention to him.

"Gawd!" Bull Badgely swore long and fervently. "That wind is fierce. Chills a feller plumb to the bone."

Melody laughed. "That's one way of keepin' a cool head, Bull."

"Huh!" Badgely grunted. Then Melody's words commenced to seep in. "Head cool?" he queried. "Who said anythin' about—sa-a-ay, Madigan, you insinooatin' I'm a bone head?"

9

"No, I wa'n't *insinuatin'*," Melody returned, grinning broadly. "Fact is, I didn't mention you in particular——"

"You better not," Badgely snarled, "not less'n you're lookin' for trouble."

Melody sobered. He hadn't intended the words to be any more than a joke, but it seemed Badgely was accepting them in a different light.

"Why, no, Badgely," Melody said slowly, "I ain't lookin' for trouble. I ain't side-steppin' any, either. As for what I said—well, if the boot fits, put it on, an' I'll see if I can find a spur for you to go with it."

"Why, damn you, Madigan!" Badgely set down his plate and started around the fire toward Melody. The next instant, his feet slid from under him and he sat down abruptly in the mud. For the first time that morning laughter broke through the grumbling. His face crimson with rage, Badgely picked himself up.

At that moment the Old Man stepped in between Melody and Badgely. "Now, look here, boys," he said soothingly, "cut out the scrappin'. They ain't no use of it, an' we've had enough trouble so far. Bull, you go on back an' finish your breakfast. Melody, you better quit hoorawin' the boys until they're better tempered." But his eyes were twinkling as he spoke the words. In a few minutes quiet was restored.

But the laughter had helped. By the time breakfast was concluded the men were all feeling better—except Bull Badgely. Bull returned to his blankets which, with those of the other men had been stowed away in the wagon, procured his bottle and drank deeply of its contents.

Along the eastern horizon a faint tinge of gray had commenced to spread. As it became lighter, the wind increased to a tornado-like velocity. It was growing colder. The gale whipped the rain and snow into faces, stinging and biting like thousands of sharpened points.

Bracing themselves against the howling fury, the punchers made their way down to the rope corral, trying to shake the kinks out of their stiff, wet ropes. Melody noticed that his gun wasn't on, started for the wagon to get it from his roll, then changed his mind and sauntered down toward the horses, deciding to get it later. That's where he made a mistake.

At the rope corral everything was in confusion. Some of the punchers were already mounted. Others were still try-

10

ing to rope their mounts. A few didn't know whether they were on or off, due to the plunging activities of their ponies. Horses dashed wildly this way and that. The sharp hoofs of the animals had churned the corral to a slushy mass of slippery gumbo.

Melody laid his saddle on the ground, and commenced shaking out a loop in his lariat. He made his way around the rim of the small herd, eyes searching for a certain little black gelding. Suddenly he released his cast.

At the same instant, Bull Badgely sent a loop toward his own mount. The ropes crossed, tangled, both men missed their marks. "Dammit!" Badgely roared in anger. "Where'd you learn to handle a throw-rope, Madigan?"

Melody coiled his rope before replying, then, "Sorry, Bull," he said easily. "I didn't aim to block your toss, only it's a mite dark yet, to see clear. Reckon, it wa'n't either of us at fault."

He didn't wait for Badgely's next remarks, but again made his throw. This time it settled true about the neck of the little cowpony, and he led it out of the herd. A few yards away, Badgely was making a second attempt, swearing harsh oaths, meanwhile.

Melody threw the blanket across his horse's back, only to have the gale almost whip it out of his hands. It was necessary to put blanket and saddle on together. This was accomplished at last, and the cinch pulled tight. The cold had put the devil in that little black's heart this morning. Melody laughed as he started to climb up. "Hol' still, yuh snake headed crowbait!"

An instant later he settled himself into the saddle, not noticing that Bull Badgely was mounting nearby. For one brief moment the black stood stock still, then its head went down between its feet, its muscles bunched and it went straight up! Up, up, up! Then down, hoofs bunched close. Nothing vicious about that bucking. The little black was just getting warmed up, that was all. Warming for Melody Madigan, too. He let out a wild cowboy yell, and commenced fanning the horse's head with his folded sombrero!

In the next thirty seconds the little horse gave everything it had. It sun-fished, swapped ends, whirled and reversed, hindquarters snapping out like the end of a blacksnake whip. Melody managed to grin and stay on,

11

his head bobbing back and forth as though fastened to an elastic neck.

It was difficult to hold the little horse down. The footing was none too good. Thus it was that Melody's horse crashed into the mount Bull Badgely was riding. There came a mad scramble of flying hoofs, mud spattered in all directions. Badgely's horse was carried off balance and for the second time that morning, Bull took a wet mud bath. He was up in an instant, uninjured. His horse scrambled to its feet. Badgely slashed it cruelly across the head with the quirt, attached to his wrist, and again mounted. His face was black with anger, his blood-shot eyes seeking out Melody among the many shadowy figures in the dim light.

By this time Madigan's black had taken to crow-hopping. Melody reined it around, trotted back to the spot where Badgely sat waiting. "I'm plumb sorry about tippin' you, Bull," Melody commenced sincerely. "This dang pup just plain outrode me for a minute——"

"You're a damn' liar!" Badgely cut in, voice hoarse with rage. "You done it a-purpose!"

Some of the men had stopped nearby and stood laughing. It didn't seem to be serious. Surely, Badgely couldn't hold an accident of that kind against Melody.

Melody slipped to the ground, dropped reins over his horse's head, and came toward Badgely. "Honest, Bull," he was saying, "I couldn't help that. I didn't know yuh was nowheres near me. Shucks, feller, nobody's hurt. Let's forget it. I've told you I'm sorry. Is there anythin' I can do to prove it?"

"Not a blasted thing!" Badgely rasped. His liquor was working now. "You set out to make a fool outta me. You called me a bonehead, you tangled my rope, and then you spill my bronc. You kinda figure I'll let you off to pull some more of them clown plays, if you pretend to be sorry, eh——"

"Use your head, Bull," Melody broke in. He was still trying to avoid a rupture, but there was a trace of irritation in his voice. "I'm not lookin' for trouble with you. This ain't the time for it. There's work to be done——"

"Damn right you ain't wantin' trouble," Badgely snarled. "You yellow——" It was a vile epithet that Badgely next voiced, the sort of language that spells "fight" any place where cow country English is understood.

Had it been broad daylight, the other punchers would

12

have seen Melody go white about the lips. The muscles at the corners of his mouth went taut. His whole form grew rigid. Fighting for control, he took one step in Badgely's direction.

"There's only one answer to a name like that, Badgely." Melody's voice was cold, harsh with strain. "Either take it back, mighty *pronto*, or fill your hand!"

The circle of men around the two had gone strangely quiet. From a short distance away sounded the Old Man's voice. He came on the run, yelling orders to Badgely and Madigan. But he arrived too late. The two men reached to hips, together. Then it was that Melody remembered he didn't have his gun on!

Bull Badgely's gun came streaking up—a crimson stab of flame tore a long slash in the gloom. For a moment there was no further sound, save the echoes of the shot and the noise made by a man's feet stumbling weakly in the mud.

"The joke's on me," they heard Melody mutter. He put out one protesting hand as though to ward off the next shots he knew would come.

They did. There was something savage in the manner in which Badgely released his next two slugs. They came close together, the illumination from the flares throwing his hate-contorted face into bold relief. Melody staggered back, spun half around. Then his legs buckled at the knees and he pitched forward on his face.

Silence for a moment. Then shouts and excited yells. The men closed in.

"I guess I taught that feller what's what!" Badgely laughed triumphantly.

"You damn' fool!" someone accused. "He didn't have no gun. It's murder, Bull, an' you deserve hangin'!"

"No gun?" Badgely's jaw dropped. "Hell! He must 'a' had. He invited it." It was light enough now to show that the man's eyes were dilated with sudden fear. "Aw, I don't believe it." Without taking the time to see, he reined his horse toward the wagon where his bottle was kept.

The Old Man was shouting orders, now. Several of the punchers ran for the corral to quiet the excited horses. Others picked up the unconscious figure in the mud and carried it gently to some blankets near the fire. For a time all was confusion in the camp.

13

Bull Badgely, drinking in the shadow of the wagon, suddenly found the bottle torn from his grasp. "Hey, that's mine," he protested.

"Try an' take it away, you coyote," came the belligerent answer from the puncher who had taken it. "Shootin' a man that ain't got a gun. I'm plumb regretful that we got to use this for Melody, but he needs it more than you do, rotten as it is."

Bull fell silent. For the present he decided it would be better not to object. The puncher disappeared with the bottle.

It was snowing harder now. The leaden skies hung low overhead. The draws were commencing to fill with drifting white. The Old Man was working feverishly over Melody. Eventually the wounded cowboy regained consciousness. He was badly hit. His eyes twitched open, and he managed a faint smile. "The joke was—on me," he gasped feebly. "Don't hold it—against Bull. I invited him to draw——"

A pinkish froth blew out through his lips as he talked, and certain snowflakes that drifted down were instantly submerged in the ragged crimson stain on his breast.

Melody was speaking again, this time to the Old Man: "Remember, now—" something fierce in the tones "—don't do nothin' to Bull. I ain't holdin' that against—him, but I'd like to see—if he could do it—again—sometime."

His eyes closed and his head rolled to one side.

"Do it again, sometime," a man repeated bitterly. "Hell! They ain't goin' to be no 'again' for Melody Madigan——"

"Yo're a liar!" The Old Man's voice was tense with strain, something of a sob in the tones. "Dammit! Lewis, there *is* goin' to be another chance for Melody. He's too good a kid to croak like this. Billings, you'n Lewis get one of them wagons hitched up and spread some blankets comfortable. Then drive like hell to the doctor's."

"Bring the doctor back?" Billings queried dumbly.

"Hell, no! Melody won't last that long. Take him—an' take him fast! You'll have me to face, if you don't get him there in time, too—— Move, damn you, move!"

Eventually, the wagon rumbled off across the range, Billings driving like one possessed. Inside, Lewis was dosing out whisky to Melody.

The punchers stood looking after the wagon in the

14

graying light until it was lost to view. One of them shivered. "Jeez, it's cold," he muttered.

The sleet cut sharp whips across their faces as they headed back toward the rope corral. . . .

## 2. Melody Rides South

SOMETIMES a rugged constitution and a life in the open air will do wonders for a man. Melody Madigan hovered between life and death for months, but finally gained the ascendancy over the Grim Old Reaper. This, only after certain complications had been checked and side-tracked by a frontier physician skilled in the treatment of gun wounds. The chinook had come and gone before Melody was able to get about to any extent, and then, only with the aid of a cane. He had lost considerable blood, and it requires time to rebuild a bullet-shattered constitution.

The boys from the Crossed-Anchors drifted into town at regular intervals to see him. Bull Badgely hadn't been arrested. Melody's words had prevented that, although the sheriff and the hands of the Crossed-Anchors never could understand why it had been necessary for Bull to send two additional slugs after that first shot. Bull had had sufficient time to see that Melody was unarmed. But Bull had pulled out of the country immediately after the close of beef roundup, and the affair hadn't been followed up.

One bright spring morning found Melody riding out to the Crossed-Anchors where he was greeted with whoops of delight. Much of his tan had disappeared, but he was feeling fit again. The Old Man gruffly shook his hand. When he and Melody were alone,

"What am I owin' you?" Melody asked.

The Old Man knew to what Melody referred, but pretended ignorance. "Owin' me? What for?"

"Doctor bills—and them two nurses you brought down from Helena—and medicine——"

"Yeah, I can put you on t'once," the Old Man cut in blandly. "Fact is, I sorta held your job open, knowin' you'd be back. Throw your things in your old bunk. Better take it easy for a few days, and——"

"Listen, I ain't working for no slave driver no more,"

16

Melody interrupted, but he smiled broadly when he said the words. "I'm driftin'."

The Old Man's eyes held wistful lights. "I wish I could go along with you and see the finish," he said, then added, "but it's your game to play out alone—in your own way. He told me he was headin' south."

"Thanks, that's somethin'. I sorta want to see," Melody explained, "if Badgely could do it again. Somehow, I got my doubts. South, eh? That's good. I was brought up in that country. Busted my first bronc in Arizona—— But, I'm repeatin', what do I owe you?"

Reluctantly, the Old Man struggled with mental calculations. A figure finally came to mind. He slashed it in two, divided it again, and mentioned a certain sum. "You can pay me, anytime," he added. "I don't need the money."

"Might as well get it off'n my mind, now," Melody said. He wrote out an order on his bank, and after some further protestations, the Old Man accepted it. He didn't know that the amount virtually wiped out Melody's savings of a lifetime.

"Badgely didn't say exactly where he was headin', eh?" Melody asked, after some further conversation.

The Old Man shook his head. "Just mentioned that he was headin' south."

Melody stayed the night at the Crossed-Anchors bunkhouse, and pulled out early the next morning.

For weeks he drifted, drawing ever closer to the Mexican Border. Occasionally, he'd stop at some outfit on his way and work for a few days, breaking horses. But he never stayed long in any one place. As he journeyed south he saw the sage turn from green to dusty gray, watched the mountains flatten out and give way to long stretches of half-desert country. The sun grew hotter.

It was getting along toward late summer, one day, when he reined his pony up the slopes of the Verde Hills, which were little more than low, round-topped mounds covered with sage, mesquite, cactus, chaparral, and other growths familiar to the southwest. He was riding a horse picked up on his travels, a small roan mare of undoubted stamina and speed.

The mare wasn't showing much speed at present, however. It was just plodding along, taking things easy in the heat of the day. Melody's chaparejos hung from the saddle. A slicker and blankets were rolled behind. His roll-brim sombrero of grayish white was tipped down over one eye. For the rest, his costume consisted of well-worn overalls, the wide cuffs of which hung halfway down to the high heels of the spurred riding boots; a dark woolen shirt; and faded vest that served solely to carry his Durham and papers. Two cartridge belts of wide leather encircled Melody's slim hips, each weighted with a holstered, single-action, Colt's forty-five.

Melody slouched in the saddle and drew mournful notes from the old accordion in his hands, the while his voice was raised in the words of a song:

> Oh, once I loved a Texas gal,
>   But she dang near druv me crazy,
> For at a dance, she wouldn't prance;
>   She was so fat and lazy.

The accordion wheezed and groaned. Melody took a deep breath and commenced the second stanza:

> So then I got a wealthy maid
>   Who lived in Albuquerque,
> But her eyes was crossed, an' me she bossed;
>   An' I wanted a wife less perky.

The little mare's ears flattened against her head, she snorted disdainfully. Melody grinned. "Get along, Jezebel. I know muh voice is terrible, but you gotta stand it." He punched violently on the instrument for the discordant notes of the third verse:

> Next, I courted a Rio miss,
>   Pretty, an' pert, an' slender;
> But she left me flat for a cholo rat
>   Who treated her more tender.

Melody's voice broke a trifle on the high-pitched strains of the final words. "Gosh, I ain't no nightingale," he mused seriously. "Mebbe that's the reason I was thrun outta the church singin' that time." His bronzed face crinkled to a grin at certain memories of the past. Further chords were squeezed from the accordion:

18

*A bachelor's life is the life for me,*
  *I'm through with gals forever;*
  *For many a skirt has done me dirt——*

Melody suddenly ceased singing, reined in the mare, and strained his ears. Again, it came, the far-off echo of a repeating rifle. Then a third report!

"That last sounded like a Colt-gun, or I'm a liar." Melody exclaimed. He dropped from the horse's back, slung the accordion back of the saddle, and started forward on foot for the crest of the hill which he had been ascending. Here, there was a thick growth of juniper which shielded his approach. Reaching the top of the hill, he found himself gazing down a long gradual slope that stretched to a broad, fertile valley, some two or three miles in length. Throughout the valley, the earth was dotted with a scattering of Hereford cows. Beyond the valley the hills were less numerous. The terrain flattened considerably, to the south.

Again came the sound of the Colt-gun. Melody's eyes shifted toward the western end of the long grassy bowl and rested on a clump of cottonwoods where a soft swirl of gray drifted through the branches. He looked closer and perceived a group of adobe buildings almost hidden among the trees.

Another shot sounded, and Melody saw two riders cut through the cottonwoods and head for more open country. They were riding fast, evidently intent on getting away from the buildings as soon as possible. The reason for the move was plainly explained by the series of shots that followed them from the house among the trees.

"Looks like somebody was mad," Melody grunted. "I dunno who's in that house, but he's sure foggin' his heat plentiful. Two Winchesters against a six-gun. Big odds, but Ol' Man Colt seems to be holdin' the fort, judgin' by the way them two waddies is fannin' their tails."

By this time the shooting had ceased. Melody's eyes followed the two riders as they came scurrying across the valley floor, too far away for him to make out their features. The pair were now following a small cottonwood-fringed stream that flowed through the center of the valley. Once out of range of the house the fleeing riders slowed pace, but kept going.

Melody dropped down on his stomach behind a juniper

bush to see if anything further happened. For a moment the two riders passed from his range of vision. His gaze strayed farther to the west, past the house and the cottonwoods, and into the foothills of the Trozar Range that lay beyond. There, the country took on a more rugged aspect, the tall, jagged peaks of the Trozars standing against the blue sky like grim sentinels above the tiny ranch buildings in the valley far below.

"H'mmm—wonder what it was all about," Melody mused. Again, he glanced down the slope. The two riders were nearer, now, something short of a mile distant. They were riding side by side, and Melody could tell by their gesticulating hands that they were conversing angrily about the exchange of shots.

There came a sudden crashing in the brush to Melody's left, and eight or ten yards below him. The next moment a slim figure in ragged overalls and run-down, flat-heeled boots pushed into view, its back to Melody. The puncher decided it was a boy, though he may have guessed wrong. The figure was too slight to be a man's, and he couldn't see the fellow's face. A battered old sombrero covered the boy's head.

Melody lay motionless, face close to the ground. He watched the boy crawl on hands and knees to the shelter of a small pile of broken rock. In one hand the slim figure in overalls trailed a rifle at his side. Melody caught an angry exclamation, as the boy raised to knees and leveled the gun across the top of the rock pile. Melody held his breath. He had a feeling that he was about to witness a killing. There was something deadly in the easy manner in which the boy adjusted the rifle sights and took cool, steady aim. Without reasoning why, Melody felt his sympathies going out to the overalled figure.

# 3. "They Want Our Outfit"

THE BOY had drawn a bead on one of the horsemen, and was just about to pull trigger, when Melody spoke: "I wouldn't, was I you, son," he advised softly.

The boy's nerve was good. No doubt about that. For a moment he didn't move a muscle, then the rifle was allowed to slowly slip to the ground, and he raised his hands in the air, before turning to face Melody.

"Why wouldn't you?" he demanded coldly.

Melody was admiring the kid's nerve. "Two reasons," he replied, "the first bein' that it'd be called murder, if yuh scored a hit—which same brings us to the second reason. That ol' Winchester of yours wouldn't stretch that far. Lord, son, them hombres is all of fifteen hundred yards away. So unless your gun is a heap better than I think, you'd just be wastin' your lead and callin' them hombres up here to investigate."

Something of relief had passed over the boy's face as his eyes first fell on Melody. "I've scored at eight hundred," he snapped.

"Which leaves a difference of some seven hundred," Melody pointed out.

He had been looking at the boy, noticed that the skin was unusually white where a bit of arm showed beneath one uprolled sleeve of the faded blue shirt. Not a bad looking kid, with his reddish hair and blue eyes. Sort of a fighting chin, too, Melody decided.

He was deciding something else when the boy broke in on his thoughts, something bitter in the tones: "I suppose you're some new gunman that Du Sang has hired. Well, what are you figuring to do with me?"

Melody grinned broadly. "If you had a dress on, I might invite you to a dance, if there was a dance handy," he replied. "You ain't a *he*, after all, are you? I figured you was too pretty to be a boy——"

"Thank heaven I'm not a man," the girl exclaimed with some heat. "Bein' a man on this range is nothin' to be proud of, with one possible exception."

"Yeah?" Melody whistled softly. "Don't like us, eh? Must be you're on the prod, kid——"

"Don't call me 'kid.' I'm nearly nineteen," she flared.

"All right, Nearly Nineteen," Melody drawled soothingly. "I'll try to remember. And just to take a load off'n your mind, I'm statin' now that I ain't been hired by—what was that name, Du Sang? An' you can take your hands down. I ain't aimin' to draw on you. Sit down, take it easy, an' tell papa how you come to bump your head. This country commences to look interestin'."

The girl smiled in spite of herself, then turned and glanced down into the valley. The two riders were some distance away by this time. She moved up the slope and seated herself a few feet distant from Melody, who had rolled over and now sat with his back against a small boulder.

"I can give you the information you're probably wondering about, in a few words," she commenced. "The Du Sang crowd is tryin' to run this country, and they come pretty close to succeeding. They want our outfit—the Rafter-S—but we don't see it that way—yet. There's just Dad and me. Dad is Tom Norris. I'm Jerry Norris—Geraldine, if you want it that way."

"Jerry suits. I'm Melody Madigan. Strange around here, though I know other parts of the Southwest. That's your place down among the cottonwoods, I take it."

Jerry Norris nodded. "Yes, Dad is down there with a broken leg. He had an argument with one of Du Sang's gunmen some time back. Dad beat the fellow to the draw, but got plugged just above the knee. He's just commencing to get around again. I wish he'd had this rifle, instead of a six-gun when those two showed up. You see, he's warned the Du Sang crowd to stay off our property."

She got to her feet. Melody also arose. "I've got to be getting along. Dad was still slinging lead when those two plug-uglies rode away, so I know he's all right, but he may be worried about me. Well, s'long, I probably won't see you again."

She started on foot down into the valley. The two riders had disappeared by this time.

"Hey, wait a minute," Melody called. Jerry stopped and

he continued, "What makes you think you won't see me again?"

"I might at that," she returned slowly, "providin' you join up with Du Sang. Otherwise, you won't be stayin' in this part of the country. Du Sang wouldn't let you."

"Oh, so that's it, eh? Uh-huh, I see—— Where's your horse?"

The girl's lips tightened. "Laying dead about a mile back. I left him for a few minutes while I headed into the brush to see if I could stir up a few quail for dinner——"

Melody's lips twitched. "With that rifle?"

"With this rifle," the girl replied shortly. "I've done it before, and I'll do it again. We don't happen to own a shotgun. This rifle and Dad's Colt is all we have——"

"And your hawss stepped into a hole and broke his leg, and you had to shoot him, eh?"

"Shoot him nothing!" the girl said heatedly. "One of those men you saw shot him! They were looking for me, too, but I kept out of sight in the brush. Then they went on to the house. Probably figured there was no one there, although they should know that Dad isn't able to ride yet."

"Nice neighborly sort, ain't they? Do you know their names?"

"One of 'em is called Manitoba, the other, Badgely. I don't——"

"Badgely? What's his first name?"

"Bull. Do you know him?"

"I've encountered him at various times," Melody replied dryly.

"He's foreman of the Diamond-8—that's the Du Sang outfit—— Well, I've got to be going. Dad's going to be plumb disappointed when I show up without any quail."

"Oh, well, you can always fall back on beans."

"Can you?" A touch of sarcasm in the tones.

Melody flushed. "Sure, I like beans—'specially when I can't get anythin' else."

Jerry Norris bit her under lip. "Some folks are like that," she nodded gravely, after a moment.

Melody changed the subject. "Wait until I get my hawss. You can ride down and get another mount, then bring the mare back to me. I'll wait here."

The girl started to refuse, then thinking better of it, kept silent. Melody had already started back toward the spot where he had left Jezebel.

He returned in a few minutes riding the mare, dropped from the saddle, and shortened the stirrup straps. Not much, though. The girl was fairly tall. Melody looked at Jerry, then at Jezebel. "I reckon she'll carry you," he said a trifle uneasily. "I'm hopin' so, anyhow. Sometimes Jezebel is a mite skeery 'round strangers."

The girl swung easily to the saddle. Luckily, the mare behaved. "I'll get back as soon as I can," Jerry Norris said, "and—and I'm much obliged."

Melody removed the accordion from the saddle and nodded. "Don't mention it, an' don't hurry on my account."

The girl rode off down the slope. Melody threw himself on the ground in the scanty shade furnished by a juniper, and commenced to roll a smoke. That finished, he took up the accordion.

He was still singing—at least Melody termed it singing —when the girl returned about an hour later, riding a big gray gelding and leading Jezebel behind. She sat her horse, something of contempt showing in her eyes.

"I wondered what those terrible noises were," she stated bluntly. "Sounded like somebody tearing rags."

Melody grinned. "You're not the first person that thought I oughta do somethin' with my voice," he answered amiably, getting to his feet.

The girl refused to become infected with his humor. "Is that all you do—travel around the country and play that bellows contraption?" she asked coldly.

"And sing," Melody reminded sweetly.

"So that's what you call it?"

"Besides ropin' a cow now and then, an' shootin' my guns to see will they go off—an' lendin' my hawss to gals that have been set a-foot."

The girl's cheeks crimsoned. "I'm sorry," she apologized icily. "I'd forgotten I was under obligations to you."

"Forget it. You're not. Is your father all right?"

Jerry Norris nodded. "Yes. He wasn't hurt. He wanted to ask you down to see him, but I told him you wouldn't come."

"You told him——" Melody commenced. Then he stopped, his eyes widening. He smiled thinly after a moment. "You thought that I was afraid to go down there with you, didn't you, on account them two hombres might come back?"

"That was the idea, wasn't it?" The tones weren't at all friendly.

Melody had had two reasons for remaining behind. He had thought that perhaps the girl wouldn't want to ride double. That was his first reason. His second: in case Badgely and the other man did return, the cowboy wanted to be in position to see them first.

The girl sat looking at him, waiting for her answer. Melody slung his accordion behind his saddle, readjusted the stirrup straps, then swung up to Jezebel's back, catching the reins as the girl released them.

"Well?" she prompted.

"Deponent sayeth not," Melody grinned. "You got your mind made up, so we'll let it ride thataway. There's two things that a man can't change, the first bein' a woman's mind."

Jerry's eyes flashed dangerously. "Yes? And what's the second, may I ask?"

"You may. The second is an *angry* woman's mind. I'm commencin' to suspicion why you don't like me, but I'm hopin' to rise in your estimation as time passes. Which way to town?"

"You'll find Vaca Wells about a seventeen mile ride east of here. Slightly southeast. You'll pick up our trail at the far end of the valley. You can't see the road from here because of those trees along the stream which you'll have to cross. Just before leaving the valley you'll find the trail to town leads down through a hollow with a deal of brush on either side. Before you get to that hollow, you'll see another trail, but that swings off to the north, farther on. But I warn you, if you go to Vaca Wells, you'll find some of that Du Sang crowd in town——"

"That's what I'm goin' there for."

"Oh!" The girl looked at him doubtfully. "They don't like strangers—unless, of course, you are planning to join them." Her voice was scornful.

"I know a stranger that don't like them, neither," Melody returned gravely. "I just want you to remember one thing." He lifted his hat. "Notice it?"

"What?" the girl asked puzzledly.

"Muh red hair. I noticed yours, first off, though yours is more coppery like, 'stead of brick like mine. Us red-heads has gotta stick together. That's what I wanted you to remember."

25

And without giving Jerry Norris an opportunity to answer, he wheeled his pony and swept off down the hillside.

The girl sat looking after him until he had disappeared among the trees in the bottom of the valley. "Now, I wonder what he meant by that," she mused. "Is it possible I misjudged him, and that he wasn't afraid at all? Darn it! I'm always saying the wrong thing. Oh, well, I'll probably never see him again, anyway. It's a good thing he didn't decide to come to the house. It'd be darn hard to stretch a couple of potatoes and one slice of bacon three ways."

# 4. "Come and Get It!"

ALTHOUGH it rejoiced in the position of county seat, Vaca Wells wasn't much of a town. It consisted of one dusty main street and two cross streets. There were several saloons, two feed stores, a livery stable, two restaurants, a clothing store, a hotel which rarely did any business, and a general store which sold practically anything that could be desired in that section of the cow country. There were also several other buildings which sheltered various commercial enterprises, hardly worth naming.

In short, Vaca Wells was the typical cowtown to be found in the Southwest of that day. Its buildings were of two kinds—low, flat-roofed structures of adobe brick mostly used as dwellings, and the business houses of frame construction, the boards of which were unpainted and warped from many seasons of scorching heat. Several of these last boasted high, false-fronts. The A. S. & T. N. Railroad had run a spur to one end of Vaca Wells, but except in the fall months, when the cattle pens were full, no train ever came there.

Melody had pushed the mare hard, and the little pony was streaked with sweat when the cowboy came riding into the town. He turned down the first cross street, then swung onto the main thoroughfare which was bordered on either side with an almost unbroken line of hitch-racks at which stood several droop-headed cowponies and three or four wagons. Melody was looking for Bull Badgely, now, but didn't see him among the few pedestrians on the plank sidewalks. Anyway, the most likely place to locate Bull would be in a saloon.

Madigan drew rein before the first saloon that met his gaze. Its false-front bore words in faded, paint-blistered letters that proclaimed it to be THE HERE'S A GO SALOON. Melody dismounted, loosened the pony's cinch, and flipped the reins over the tie-rail. A moment later, his high-heeled boots clumped across the plank walk to the wooden-awninged porch that fronted the building. Then, he pushed on, through the open doorway.

The interior of the saloon was dim and cool after the broiling sun-glare of the street. Along the right-hand wall, as Melody entered, was the bar. To the cowboy's left were three wooden tables and some chairs. At the back of the low-ceilinged room was a closed door.

Only one man stood at the bar, a swarthly-faced fellow in puncher attire with beady black eyes and a brilliant scarlet neckerchief knotted at his throat. His hair, under a high-crowned sombrero, was black and coarse and hung down across a narrow forehead to brush his bushy eyebrows. Probably a touch of Indian or Mexican blood in the man. There was a gun at each hip, the holsters of which were efficiently tied down with strips of rawhide.

At one of the tables ranged along the left wall, a man who appeared to be a tramp was slumped down in a chair, his eyes closed in slumber. He was ragged, unkempt, dirty. Flies crawled in and out of his open, snoring mouth.

It was the bartender Melody noticed most. The barkeep was probably the fattest individual on whom Melody had ever laid eyes. He was a man of around forty years of age, with a shock of light hair plentifully besprinkled with silver. There was something kindly in his blue-eyed gaze as he waddled to Melody's end of the bar to take the cowboy's order.

"Howdy, cowpoke," he grunted in genial tones. "What you drinkin'?"

"Got any cold beer?"

"Migawd! Where'd we get the ice?"

"I'll take warm beer, then."

To all appearances, Melody was ignorant of the suspicious glances cast at him by the man with the scarlet neckerchief. He sipped the luke-warm beer slowly, and when the glass was empty, the fat bartender set up the drinks.

"Ridin' or stoppin', stranger?" the swarthy-browed man queried after a time.

"That depends," Melody drawled.

"On what?"

"On me an' my hawss."

"Oh, I see." But it was plain that the questioner didn't

28

see at all. A frown creased his forehead as he gazed at Melody, scarcely knowing what to say next.

Melody tossed some coins on the bar. "Let's have some settin'-up exercises, again, barkeep. I reckon we're all thirsty enough to indulge once more."

The bartender took the orders. Melody noticed that the tramp sitting in the corner was still asleep. "That dude slepin', a prohibitionist?" Melody asked.

The bartender laughed, then called, "Hey, Jug-Handle, this gent is buyin'." He turned again to Melody. "He drifted in here 'bout a week back. He does my reddin' up mornin's, an' watches the bar while I'm at meals. Otherwise, I reckon him an' work has had a fallin' out—— Jug-Handle! can't you hear?"

The tramp awoke and shuffled up to the bar, looked inquiringly at the bartender. "The gent's buyin' a drink," the bartender explained a second time.

The tramp looked gratefully at Melody, then croaked, "Lightnin', Pee-Wee."

The swarthy man in the scarlet neckerchief looked somewhat put out. "Mostly, down here," he hinted, "hombres is particular who they sluice down with."

Melody nodded. "I don't like to drink with strangers, myself," he replied, purposely misconstruing the other's statement. "My name's Melody Madigan."

The bartender performed introductions, after shaking hands with Madigan. "I'm Pee-Wee Page, owner of this parlor of thirst. You heard Jug-Handle's name. Madigan, this gent is Manitoba Somethin'-or-Other. If he's got another name, nobody ever heard it."

"An' nobody ever will," Manitoba smiled thinly and thrust out his hand toward Melody. Melody, at that moment, happened to be rolling a cigarette and didn't see the proffered paw, although somehow he managed to shake hands with Jug-Handle. He was remembering now, that Jerry Norris had named Manitoba as one of the two riders down in the valley. He wondered where Badgely was. The drinks were consumed.

"Where you from, Madigan?" Manitoba asked after a time.

"Montana, recently. Arizona, originally."

"No work in Montana?"

"Plenty. Thought I'd drift down and look over my home range. Picked up a few dollars bustin' broncs on the way down. Mebbe I'll get work here, an' mebbe I won't. Anythin' else you'd like to know?" A smile accompanied the words, but there was nothing of humor in Melody's eyes.

Manitoba's face reddened a trifle. "Yeah, there is," he said doggedly. "What's your idea of stoppin' here?"

"I was thirsty."

"Hell! You know what I mean. We like to know who's comin' here."

"Who's 'we'?"

"Why—er—the town, of course."

"When the town presents its proper credentials in a body," Melody drawled, "I'll be furnishin' further information."

Pee-Wee Page was commencing to look uneasy. The tramp glanced at the two, curiosity in his grimed features. Manitoba's narrow brow furrowed into deep creases. He couldn't decide whether to become angry, or not. Certainly, Madigan hadn't revealed the information Manitoba was seeking. On the other hand, this strange cowboy was so good-natured appearing that Manitoba couldn't bring himself to believe that Madigan was openly defying him. Manitoba decided to try once more. A new suspicion had entered his mind.

"Say," he demanded suddenly, "are you a Cattle Association man?"

Melody hesitated just the right length of time before answering: "Well, what if I am?"

"There's been two of them snoopin' dicks down here within the past six months," Manitoba answered meaningly, a certain veiled menace in the words. "The first one left plumb sudden. The second—never did leave. The sheriff couldn't nohow learn who plugged him."

Melody yawned indolently. "Some counties," he drawled, "is plumb unfortunate in electin' them kind of sheriffs."

Manitoba's eyes glittered. "I ask a question," he half-snarled, "an' I want an answer plenty pronto. Are you a dick, or ain't you?"

Melody laughed softly. "Danged if you ain't the questionest hombre I ever see. Just to be contrary, I ain't answerin' one way or the other. If you insist on anythin' else, come an' get it!"

As he finished speaking, the cowboy's right hand dropped carelessly and hooked one thumb in his gun-belt, fingers spread near holster.

Manitoba moved involuntarily to meet the challenge, then checked himself. For the first time he'd noticed that Madigan's eyes had gone hard and cold. Something about those eyes Manitoba didn't like—frozen flames of fire leaping in their depths. For one brief moment Manitoba met that steely gaze, then suddenly it was borne in upon him that he had met one who could be, if occasion demanded, as much of a killer as himself.

A strange shiver of fear ran along Manitoba's spine. He could feel the hair ruffling at the back of his neck. His courage suddenly evaporated. It oozed out in the cold perspiration that dotted his forehead. He backed away a pace, eyes dropping before Melody's steady gaze.

"Aw, shucks, Madigan," he muttered uneasily, "I ain't aimin' to make trouble. You got me wrong——"

Melody shook his head. "No, I didn't judge you wrong, Manitoba, but I do know you ain't lookin' for trouble—right now. Your game is shootin' hawsses, I figure—or rather, a certain hawss on the Rafter-S range——"

"What—what—" Manitoba commenced in startled tones.

"An' mebbe I should add, makin' war on a gal an' a man with a broken leg," Melody pursued relentlessly. "Where's Bull Badgely?"

The question came so suddenly, it almost took Manitoba's breath away. "Why, Bull's right here in town," he replied in surprise. "You know him?"

Melody nodded. "Yeah—but I hope Vaca Wells won't hold it against me. Tell Bull I'll be here for a while, in case he feels like renewin' old acquaintances."

"I'll do that, Madigan," Manitoba nodded eagerly, now anxious to escape. "I was just goin' out to look for him. He's around town some place. I'll find him." The words were still tumbling from his lips as he hastened to the open doorway. The next instant he had disappeared into the street.

# 5. A Coyote's Game

A LONG SIGH of relief escaped Pee-Wee Page's lips. Jug-Handle looked curiously at Madigan, something of admiration in his dull eyes. Melody turned back to the bar to find Pee-Wee uncorking a bottle which, together with a glass, he placed on the bar. "That's the best the house affords, cowboy," Pee-Wee said mournfully. "Drink long and deep."

Melody looked at the whisky, then at Pee-Wee. "What's the idea?"

"Helpin' to speed the partin' guest," Pee-Wee explained moodily. "You're due to take a long journey, Madigan. Mebbe, if you're lucky an' don't lose no time, you can make it on your horse."

"Meanin'?"

"Meanin' that you've made an enemy of Manitoba—the meanest cuss on the Diamond-8 spread. There's enough Injun in him so he won't forget."

"Yeah?" Melody smiled easily. "He didn't look so plumb poisonous a few minutes back."

Pee-Wee mopped the perspiration from his brow. "That's because you took him by surprise. You led him up to it so easy like, that he could hardly believe his mind, when it happened. You better cross leather, son, and drift as fast as your bronc will carry you. Behind Manitoba is the hull Du Sang outfit, too——"

"I'm stayin'," Melody announced abruptly, "but I'll accept your hospitality, anyway." He tilted the bottle above his glass and poured a neat "two fingers."

Again, that flicker of admiration flitted across Jug-Handle's eyes. Melody shoved the bottle along to the tramp, but Pee-Wee seized it first and placed it under the bar. Jug-Handle muttered words of disappointment, shrugged his shoulders, and returned to the chair in the corner where he promptly fell asleep.

Melody shrewdly sized up the proprietor of the Here's A Go for a few moments, then nodded his head. "Your body may be fat, but your brain ain't" he concluded. "I'm goin' to tell you a story, then I want the lay of the land around here."

Pee-Wee bent nearer and listened closely while Melody related what he had seen from the hilltop above the Rafter-S valley, his meeting with Jerry Norris, and so on.

"In the first place," Pee-Wee stated when Melody had finished, "I thought Badgely and Manitoba were liars when they first come in here. They was both boilin' mad. Said they'd dropped over to the Rafter-S to ask for a drink of water, and without no warnin' a-tall, Tom Norris had opened fire on them. Both them coyotes swore they never even fired a shot."

"I heard the rifles crackin' before the forty-five got tuned up."

"I'm believin' you," Pee-Wee nodded angrily. "Now, I'll give you an idea of how things stand around here. There's quite a few ranches in this section of the country that do their tradin' in Vaca Wells, ship their beef, and so on, but only four of 'em is close enough to make it worth while mentionin'. In the first place, you know where Norris' Rafter-S is located. Norris' range extends considerable miles north of Verde Hills—them that borders the valley on the north—but I bet you didn't see none of his cows there."

"Only beef I saw bearin' the Rafter-S mark was right in the valley—they wouldn't make up such a big herd, neither."

"It's all that's left," Pee-Wee said, a trace of anger in his tones. "Norris didn't even bother to gather beef-stock last fall—— but I'll get on with my story. Directly south of here, about twenty miles, is George Vaughn's Lazy-V spread. Twelve miles to the east is Buck Kirby's Slash-O. You'll meet both of them owners in time—providin' you stay an' survive your meetin' with the Du Sang crowd."

"Which same I'm expectin' to do," Melody smiled gravely.

"Anticipation is often the sole joy of realization," Pee-Wee stated sourly. "I'm wishin' you luck. You'll need it. The Diamond-8 is located 'bout thirty miles west of Vaca Wells—slightly southwest—and is owned by the three Du Sang brothers. A hard trio, them three. Hugo Du Sang is

33

sort a chief of the gang, you might say. His younger brother, Guy, considers himself somethin' of a lady-killer. Then there's Luke, who's about five years older than Hugo. Luke is more interested in stowin' away liquor than anythin' else, and leaves the managin' of things to Hugo——"

"An' Hugo manages with an eye to Diamond-8 profits, from all I hear."

"Exactly. I've told you about Manitoba who is pure killer—nothin' less—and his gun-butts is notched plentiful. He'd shoot from the dark—in the back—any way, just so he'd get you. Hugo wouldn't never shoot a hombre without givin' him a square break on the draw. He's so fast, he can afford to. But I'm tellin' you now, Madigan, that I'd a thousand times rather have Manitoba for an enemy, than I would Hugo Du Sang. That's what I think of Hugo. When he makes up his mind to do somethin', hell an' high water can't stop him. And, of course, the Diamond-8 has got some other hard hombres, includin' Bull Badgely who you seem to know—I guess that's all."

Melody looked Pee-Wee steadily in the eyes, slowly shook his head. "No, it's not all," he denied. "I'm much obliged for the landscapin' information an' thumb-nail biographies, but you know damn' well that's not what I want."

Pee-Wee squirmed. Perhaps, considering his bulk, it is better to say that he quivered. "Gawd, Madigan," he said hoarsely, "it ain't safe for me to say no more. Me, I'm gettin' too fat to handle a gun fast or ride——"

"Look here," Melody cut in sternly, "it looks a heap to me as if the Rafter-S wasn't gettin' a square deal around here. If you ain't got a jellyfish for a spine, Pee-Wee, you'll come across. I'm not in the habit of spillin' everythin' I know, so anythin' you say is safe with me. 'Course, if you've got so fat an' lazy that you don't care if a girl gets tromped on, why just keep still. I'll get what I want from someone else——"

He broke off suddenly, and wheeled to glance at Jug-Handle who had ceased snoring. As he had half suspected, the tramp's eyes were only partially closed, and he was listening in on every word of the conversation. As Melody turned, the snoring was resumed. The cowboy swung back to Pee-Wee.

The big barkeep was pale as death. He forced a weak, sickly smile. "All right, Madigan," he admitted at last, "mebbe I have been layin' down an' lettin' the Diamond-8 crew run things. Naturally, I couldn't stop it alone, but if you're takin' a hand in the deal, well—" and he sighed deeply with evident resignation "a man can't die only once. Hell's bells! I might as well tell you what I know."

He gathered his thoughts and then continued. "The four ranches I mention claim to have been losin' cattle from time to time. The last coupla years, though, the thieves have sorta been concentratin' on the Rafter-S while they let up on the Slash-O and Lazy-V. To cut the story short, there seems to be plans to wipe out the Norris outfit——"

"The thieves bein' the Du Sang outfit, of course. The Diamond-8 would be li'ble to claim they was losin' cows, just to divert suspicion from themselves," Melody interrupted.

"Them's my personal sentiments, but there ain't one bit of proof to back it up," Pee-Wee answered earnestly. "They's been two range dicks down here. You heard Manitoba say what happened to them, although there's some that think the second detective shot hisself by accident."

"Do you believe that?"

"Not none! Now, here's somethin' to think about. The Latigo River rises back in the foothills of the Trozars, some place, flows east across one corner of the Diamond-8 holdings, then swings over to the valley where the Rafter-S is situated. Time was, when there was enough water for both outfits, but rivers, like female women, is prone to queer idees, sometimes. Last few years, when the hot spell sets in, the Latigo has taken to sinkin' into the earth, runnin' under-ground for a ways, and then comin' out again on Rafter-S range. Sounds funny, but——"

"Not so funny at that," Melody put in. "There's a river over near Benson—the San Pedro—that pulls one of them underground stunts, now and then, only it usually happens in flood season."

Pee-Wee nodded. "Well, anyway, the Diamond-8 has been gettin' less an' less water every year, and the Du Sangs is plumb peeved about it. Consequently, instead of hirin' an engineer an' some labor to make things right, Hugo Du Sang has started out to get the Rafter-S. First, he offered to buy it, but the money he offered was so little that nobody in their correct senses could blame Norris for refusin' to sell. Now, Du Sang is out to starve Norris out of his holdin's. The Rafter-S cows is disappearin' fast, but Norris is stubborn an' is holdin' on. He had to let all of his help go about a year ago, before beef roundup come. No money for salaries. Now, the Emporium General Store has shut down on his grub———"

"No money for grub, either, eh?"

"Oh, Norris had a few dollars that him and his daughter could live on, but it allus happens that Hardscrapple— he owns the Emporium—is just out of whatever Norris needs, when the girl drives in for supplies."

Melody's eyes blazed. "So that's Du Sang's game, eh? Damn him for a stinkin' coyote!"

"There's no proof, except that Hardscrapple is the sort that would do anythin' that Du Sang told him to do, providin' Du Sang paid him for it. I'm merely tellin' you how things look to me. For all I actually *know*, Du Sang may be as pure as the lily in the dell."

"Yeah—tiger lily," Melody exclaimed heatedly. "How about———" He broke off suddenly, then, "Beans! Now, I know what she meant by sayin' some people liked beans! Why, the poor kid didn't have nothin' to eat in the house."

"Beans?" Pee-Wee inquired blankly. "Beans? What you sayin'?"

Melody shook his head impatiently and frowned. "Nothin', Pee-Wee. Beans is what I carry under my hat in place of brains every now and then. But what about the Slash-O and Lazy-V outfits? Are they standin' for Du Sang—we'll lay it to Du Sang, until proof to the contrary shows up—runnin' a game like this on a lone man and a girl? If so, what's wrong with 'em?"

Pee-Wee scratched his head reflectively. "We-ell, I dun-no," he replied dubiously. "It's possible they don't know about it. Folks ain't riskin' Du Sang's enmity by takin' up other folks' quarrels, and since their cattle has been let alone, George Vaughn and Buck Kirby ain't paid much attention to things that's goin' on. Kirby is gettin' along in years, and he don't mix much. Vaughn ain't got only a small spread, an' he ain't no mixer, neither. Englishman. Lotsa education, I'd say, from the little I've heard him talk. Good drinker, when he comes to town, but don't take to Bourbon."

"Uh-huh. Say, Pee-Wee, is there any place around town, I can hire a buck-board?"

"Blue Star Livery, down the street a way, has one they hire out occasional. What you wantin' a wagon for?"

"I figure to take some supplies out to Norris tonight."

"Oh, migawd!" Pee-Wee staggered back, clasping his forehead. His eyes were dilated, his mouth hanging open in dumb amazement. Finally, he said slowly, "Son, did you ever hear that yarn about Daniel in the lions' den?"

"Year. Read it in the Bible once. Daniel sure had them lions hawgtied, proper."

"Uh-huh, he did. But just remember, son, you ain't no Daniel! An' what them Du Sang lions is goin' to do to you and your load of supplies is plenty. You'll never get through!"

A sigh, starting somewhere down in his toes, parted Pee-Wee's lips as he reached under the bar and produced an old forty-five, long since rusted from disuse. "Well, I might as well start cleanin' up ol' Betsy Ann," he grunted. "If you got your mind made up, I might as well go along."

Melody chuckled. "I reckon not, Pee-Wee. Ten to one the livery ain't got no two-ton wagons, and I wouldn't wanta bust down."

Pee-Wee snorted, his face became crimson, then he grinned and thrust out a hand which Melody grasped warmly. "You're right, son. An elephant would just be in the way——"

" 'Tain't that," Melody protested earnestly. "I was just kiddin'. Only, so long as you don't take sides, you'll be able to hear things. You're too valuable to lose. An' don't be worryin' about me. I figger to tie some knots in the Du Sang lions' tails!"

# PART II

# *Badgely Goes Gunnin'*

## *6.*

AFTER leaving the Here's A Go, Manitoba lost no time looking for Bull Badgely. He found Bull standing at the bar in the Silver Spur Saloon, slightly the worse for drink.

The Silver Spur was a low-ceilinged, dingy-looking place, operated by one of the Diamond-8's former punchers whom Hugo Du Sang had set up in business. There were about a dozen men in the bar when Manitoba arrived.

Badgely greeted him with open arms. "What kept you so long, Manitoba?" he asked thickly. "You know I hates to drink alone. Whatcha havin'?"

"Gimme a touch, Spurling," Manitoba told the bartender. Drinks were consumed, then Manitoba dragged the reluctant Badgely away from the bar to a table at the opposite side of the room.

"Do you happen to know a hombre by the name of Madigan—Melody Madigan——" Manitoba commenced.

Badgely gasped. A cigarette dropped from his open mouth. "Madigan, did—you—say?"

Manitoba grunted. "I see you do. Well, he's in Vaca Wells. Furthermore, he saw us out to the Rafter-S, and ——" He broke off abruptly, as his eyes lighted on the door. "Here's Hugo, now."

Hugo Du Sang had just entered the Silver Spur. With him were two of his punchers, Humphrey Tracy, known as "Hump," and Gus Randle.

Du Sang was a big man, standing well above six feet, with wide shoulders, a deep chest, and beneath his broad-brimmed Stetson a tawny mass of hair. His pale blue eyes were set too close together, and sweeping yellow mustaches partly covered a loose-lipped disagreeable mouth. He was clad in high-heel riding boots, bat-wing chaparejos, and a heavy woolen shirt. A pair of ivory-butted forty-fives hung low on his thighs.

He came at once to tahe table where Manitoba and Badgely sat. He and his men took chairs. The other two nodded. "Well?" Du Sang asked abruptly.

"It didn't work, Hugo," Manitoba said in low tones. "We'd no sooner got close to the house than I slipped a thirty-thirty at Norris who was standin' in his doorway. I missed my shot, and so did Bull. Then Norris slammed the door and opened up with his six-gun from a window. He made it sorta hot, so we sloped before he could get our range."

Du Sang's eyes narrowed, but he said nothing beyond, "Was the girl there?"

Badgely shook his head. "We found her horse, though, and I plugged it. We sorta looked around for the girl, but I reckon she was hid in the brush. We didn't look long, though, 'cause we wanted to get to the house——"

"You damn' fools!" Du Sang's voice was tense with rage. "Ain't I told you not to touch that girl? We don't want no women mixed into our play. Folks might turn against us, if we go monkeyin' with skirts. Did you come straight to town, then?"

Manitoba nodded. "We stopped at the Here's A Go for one drink. Then I stayed, while Bull come here to wait. I hinted around to Pee-Wee Page about sellin' his place, but he didn't seem agreeable. 'Course, I didn't make no reg'lar offer, 'cause you said you just wanted to get a line on——"

"He'll have to sell, that's all," Du Sang growled. "He's too damn' neutral. Folks in this neck of the range has got to be for Du Sang, or get out! I give him his chance to be friendly, but he never warmed up, so—one way or another —the fat slob has to go!"

Manitoba continued his story, told Du Sang of Madigan's arrival and of what had happened. This time Du Sang listened without interruption.

Finally, when Manitoba had finished, "You're a pair of blunderin' fools," Du Sang stated abruptly. "I told you I didn't want no outsiders to see you two at the Rafter-S."

"Hell's bells!" Badgely protested sullenly. "How was we to know Madigan was hid up in that juniper? You didn't tell us to comb the country——"

"You're expected to know some things without bein' told," Du Sang sneered. "And then, to top things, this

40

Madigan hombre puts the bee on Manitoba at the Here's A Go. I got one hell of an outfit, I have." He calmed a trifle. "You know this Madigan, eh, Bull?"

Badgely nodded. "I nearly wiped him out once," he boasted. He told the story, neglecting to state, however, that Melody had been unarmed at the time. As foreman of the Diamond-8—a position he held due to the fact that none of Du Sang's other men wanted the responsibility—Badgely knew he'd have to make his position as strong as possible, if he expected to retain his prestige. The Diamond-8 had no place for a weakling.

By the time he had finished talking, Badgely had risen in the estimation of Manitoba and the two punchers. Du Sang merely nodded, and was noncommittal in his opinion.

"I'm handin' it to you, Bull," Manitoba said frankly. "To tell the truth, I was so took by surprise that I didn't feel like pullin' on that damn' red-head—right then. Madigan's easy ways threw me off guard, and them gray eyes of his'n sorta bored right into me. 'Course, I'm a better man than he is, and I'll get him in time."

"You sure of that?" Bull asked skeptically.

"Why not?" Manitoba answered. "You admitted, yourself, Bull, that I'm faster'n you, and if you can down Madigan, I can, too. And I'll make him stay down."

"Hoof and mouth disease is what you two have got," Du Sang growled. "You hoof around town tellin' each other what wonderful guys you are, but when I give you a job you bungle it."

Hump and Gus Randle laughed loudly at Du Sang's words. Manitoba and Badgely subsided into a sullen silence. Du Sang called for a round of drinks which was served at the table, then asked Manitoba:

"What makes you think Madigan is a cattle detective?"

" 'Cause he wouldn't admit that he wasn't."

"That's no reason." Du Sang turned to Badgely. "Did you ever hear of Madigan doin' any work of that kind?"

Badgely slowly shook his head. "An' I don't think he's no dick, now, either. He was still laid up, when I left Montana. In fact, at that time they didn't think he'd pull through. I'll bet he didn't stir around much until just this spring, and we're into August now. If he got a job snoopin', he just got it recent."

"That's my idea," Du Sang agreed. "Manitoba, you take too much for granted. Mebbe this hombre is lookin' for a

41

job. If he is, I'll take him on. If he could make Manitoba back down, he's got somethin' we need."

"All right," Manitoba grunted. "What's to do?"

"Keep your hat on and let me do the thinkin'," Du Sang said curtly. "Hump and Gus drove in for a bill of supplies. I forked my bronc in, to pick you two up, before you got drunk to celebrate the rubbin' out of Tom Norris. Drunks always talk too much. Howsomever, you failed, but it's a good idea I come in, anyhow, before you pulled some more fool plays. I'll go over to the Emporium with the boys and pay Hardscrapple my bill. When we come back, I'll tell you what I've got in mind. And you two stay sober, see?"

Without another word he rose and left the saloon, followed by Tracy and Randle.

Bull Badgely slumped down in his chair, head sunk on his chest, eyes staring vacantly into space. Learning of Melody's presence in Vaca Wells had been something of a shock to him. By this time the effects of the liquor he had taken had worn off.

Manitoba sneered. "Somethin' seems to be botherin' you, Bull. Kinda put out about Madigan bein' here, ain't you?"

Badgely roused himself with an effort. "Hell, no! I ain't worryin' none about him." But his words lack the force of conviction.

"That time you plugged him," Manitoba pursued, "you didn't do it from behind, did you, Bull? Somehow, you seem to have lost your confidence."

"Aw, let's forget it and have a drink."

"Go ahead, if you got the urge. The chief said to stay sober, an' I ain't triflin' with his orders." The two men fell into silence.

It was nearly sundown when Du Sang and the two punchers returned to the Silver Spur. Du Sang looked sharply at the two waiting men, saw they were sober, and nodded with satisfaction. By this time, most of the saloon's customers had drifted out to the street, and Spurling, the bartender, was half asleep on a high stool which stood at the far end of the bar.

Du Sang came immediately to the business in hand, speaking directly to Badgely: "You're goin' to have a chance to finish what you started before, Bull," he announced, "providin' this Madigan hombre ain't warm-like

42

to reason. Hump and Gus can wait here, while you and me and Manitoba drift down to the Here's A Go. I figger to offer Madigan a job. If he don't see it that way, Bull, it's up to you to show us how fast you are."

Badgely turned a sickly green. "Well—er—say, lookit here, Hugo, do you think it's right to throw the job on me —alone?"

A scornful laugh left Manitoba's lips. Hump and Gus Randle looked curiously at their foreman. Du Sang's brows gathered to a frown. "What's wrong?" he demanded. "You afraid of Madigan?"

"Nope," Badgely gulped, "only you see, Hugo, this Madigan is fast. He always beat me shootin' in contests up in Montana——"

"Contests ain't real shootin'," Du Sang cut in. "You done it once, Bull, and you can do it again. I dunno what's got into you. You're a purty fair foreman, but seems like you've lost your nerve. You're goin' to go through with this or get off'n the Diamond-8. Make your choice and make it damn' sudden!"

Badgely reached a sudden decision. He rose abruptly to his feet. "All right. As you say, I done it once, and I can do it again. Lemme get a drink first."

He made his way to the bar, called to Spurling, and got a bottle of whisky and a glass. The others joined him. But Badgely didn't stop with one drink. He swallowed four, one right after the other. Then, he lurched toward the doorway. "C'mon," he said hoarsely, the raw liquor sending new courage flowing through his veins. "I can do it."

Tracy and Randle remained in the saloon. Hugo Du Sang and Manitoba followed Badgely to the street. It was dark when the three men stepped to the sidewalk. There weren't many people abroad.

Badgely halted a moment to inspect his equipment. He ran his fingers expertly over the tied-down holsters, then spun the Colts' cylinders to see that all was in good mechanical order. The effect of the whisky he had swallowed was rapidly whipping him into an insensate rage.

"In case he beats you to the draw, Bull," Du Sang was saying, "me'n Manitoba will be right behind you. If one can't get him, three of us can."

Badgely slammed his guns back into holsters, turned fiercely on his chief. "I ain't needin' you two," he sneered.

"I'll show you shootin' as is shootin'! Keep outta this, see? Madigan's my meat, and I aim to have his heart for supper!"

Even Du Sang quailed a trifle before the bloodlust in Badgely's eyes. "Look here, Bull," he protested, "my plan was to offer Madigan a job, first——"

Now that he was drunk again, Badgely said things he would never have dreamed of saying while sober. "Your plans ain't my plans," he rasped. "The Diamond-8 wouldn't be big enough to hold Madigan and me both. So, keep outa this, Du Sang. I know what I'm doin'."

He turned and started at a swift walk toward the Here's A Go. Manitoba reached out a hand to detain him, but with a snarl, Badgely shook him off.

"Let him go," Du Sang said quietly. "I know his type. Whisky courage, but he ain't drunk. Just savage, that's all. An' he'll be ripe to shoot like hell!"

Manitoba nodded. "I'd hate to be facin' him myself, right now."

They stood watching Badgely as the man progressed toward the Here's A Go. Squares and oblongs of yellow light showed from buildings all along the darkened street. For just an instant Du Sang and Manitoba saw Badgely pause in one of the patches of light and whip out his guns. Then, the whisky-lashed man proceeded toward the doorway of the Here's A Go.

"Geez!" Manitoba exclaimed. "Bull's pulled his irons a'ready. He ain't figurin' to give Madigan a chance. Look at him——"

Du Sang ripped out a violent oath. "Whisky-soaked fool!" he growled. "He ain't got the brains of a pack mule——"

Manitoba started forward. "Mebbe I can stop Bull before he reaches the Here's A Go——"

Du Sang flung out one hand, seized Manitoba's arm. "Let him go," he ordered shortly. "I been thinkin'—if Madigan and Bull was enemies up no'th, it's a cinch that Madigan wouldn't fit into my payroll, even if he'd hire on with me——"

"But, good Cripes, Hugo, Bull ain't givin' him a chance. Not that I care, but Vaca Wells will call it murder, shore as hell——"

"Do you think I give a damn about that?" snarled Du Sang. "Madigan come here, lookin' for trouble. Anybody

44

that ain't for me, has got to get out—one way or t'other. What if it is murder? I can square things with the sheriff. Madigan can't buck my outfit. What he's goin' to get, he asked for. Manitoba, you can say good-bye to Mr. Fresh-Guy Madigan, right now. He's on his way out!"

# 7. Flaming Lead

IN THE Here's A Go, Melody was still standing at the bar, talking to Pee-Wee Page. A few customers, having already eaten, had dropped in for their after-supper drinks.

Melody ground a cigarette butt under his heel. "It's 'bout time," he announced, "that I took on some reinforcements."

Pee-Wee looked serious. "You'll need plenty," leaning across the bar to speak in a voice that was barely audible. "You ain't no idee what you're buckin', Madigan."

Melody grinned. "I wa'n't thinkin' of that, Slim. I meant reinforcements for my stomach—chow, grub, chuck——"

"A steak by any other name would be as sweet." Pee-Wee's brow cleared a trifle. "Speakin' of steaks, don't eat at the Chink's restaurant. His other grub is all right, but his beef is so tough that it's plumb li'ble to r'ar up from your plate an' bite you first, if you ain't lookin'."

"Ain't interested in steaks," Melody said. "My palate's sort of cravin' ham-and-aigs."

Pcc-Wee looked dubious. "Eggs in this town is mostly risky," he pointed out.

"Risky?"

"You get the idee," Pee-Wee nodded gravely. "You're a heap likely to get chicken instead. Last egg I broke open on my plate, a rooster riz up and crowed right in my face. I raised hell with the restaurant proprietor an' he brung me another egg. Damn if they wa'n't a rooster in that 'un, too. Well, sir, them two birds put on the purtiest cock fight you ever see——"

"I like a good liar," Melody broke in darkly, "but you plumb outrage all sense of decency with such talk——"

"Don't you believe me?" Pee-Wee assumed an injured expression.

" 'Bout them two roosters a-ruckusin' on your plate? Oh, shore." Melody dismissed that phase of the conversation with a careless wave of one hand. "That's easy to understand. Happened to me, more'n once. Bein' boiled in his shell thataway, always raises a rooster's temper to a fightin'-mad pitch. Nope, I wa'n't thinkin' of that. What I'm objectin' to is your lack of civic pride."

"Civic pride?" Pee-Wee looked blank.

Melody nodded. "Slanderin' a fellow tradesman in such fashion. Do you think it helps business if you spread it around that fights occur durin' meal hours in this feller's eatin' house?"

"Aw, you go to hell," Pee-Wee growled genially. He started to laugh. His gaze strayed to the saloon entrance. Abruptly, his face sobered, went ashen. His lips moved futilely. Words wouldn't come. One hand raised protestingly.

Melody stared at the fat barkeep. From the doorway came an animal-like snarl of hate. Melody whirled around to see Bull Badgely lurching through the doorway, a leveled gun in either hand!

"Want me, eh, Madigan?" Badgely paused just inside the entrance and laughed crazily. "Well, here I am, comin' to finish what I started last year. Draw, damn you, draw your irons!"

Melody caught all of the picture in a single glance: the blood-shot, red-rimmed eyes, half-open mouth, bearded, hate-contorted face, the twin black muzzles of the Colt guns covering his body. Even as Badgely's harsh tones rasped through the room, Melody caught an ominous double-click, as the man thumbed back his hammers!

The customers of the Here's A Go had elevated their arms at Badgely's first words. There came the quick movements of footsteps carrying them away from the bar. Pee-Wee Page's face had turned to a sickly greenish-yellow.

Melody stood steady, like a statue graven from living marble, his gaze riveted on Bull Badgely. His arms were wide from his sides. Every nerve quivered. He had but one chance and that——

"Draw, dammit, draw!" Badgely's voice was high-pitched, shaking. "Go for your gun! I won't pull trigger, Madigan, 'til you've touched gunbutts. They said if I got you once, I could do it a second time. I will, too!" His upper lip curled back, exposing tobacco-stained fangs in a murderous grin. He went on, "Skeered, eh? Skeered to draw against Bull Badgely. I'll plug you, anyhow, you——"

Melody had suddenly flung himself to one side, left hand darting to holster. Badgely's guns roared, but Melody was moving too fast to provide a good target. The cowboy's gun streaked out, up, halted abruptly in a burst of smoke and flame!

As Melody struck the plank floor, he released a second spurt of flaming lead. Lances of orange fire had been crashing from Badgely's guns, but his bullets were finding only the back wall of the saloon.

Abruptly, an expression of shocked surprise spread over Badgely's features. His body sagged. The guns wavered uncertainly in his hands. Then, the weapons clattered to the floor. Badgely dropped to his knees, still not quite understanding what had happened. Slowly, he crumpled, face-down, on top of his weapons. A quiver ran through his form, and he lay still.

Melody rose to his feet, glanced quickly about the room. His gaze came to rest on the silent form of Bull Badgely. "I sort of wondered if he could do it again," Melody said quietly. He punched out the empty shells in his gun, blew the curling smoke from the muzzle, and replenished the empty cylinder chambers with fresh loads from his cartridge belts.

"Gawd! That was fast!" one of the customers exclaimed, something of awe in his face. Everyone commenced talking at once. The smoke drifted through the open doorway.

"I swear you'll be the death of me, yet, Melody," Pee-Wee gasped. "I can't stand no more shocks of this kind."

Melody's face was grim as he glanced down at Badgely's silent figure. "That's one of the things I sorta counted on doin' when I come down here," he said slowly, "but I didn't expect it would happen so soon." He paused a moment, frowning, then, "There's somethin' back of this. I know Bull Badgely. He wouldn't start things 'thout he had backin' of some kind. Wonder where that Manitoba hombre is?"

He moved rapidly across the floor, taking up a position just inside the doorway, and to one side. His gun swung in a swift arc that covered the room. "Not a word from any of you. Somebody else may be honin' for trouble. I crave to see 'em first."

The sounds of footsteps were heard outside. Du Sang entered, followed by Manitoba. Du Sang's jaw dropped as he noticed the body on the floor. He glanced quickly over

48

the assembled men, eyes searching for Madigan. Both he and Manitoba had passed within a few yards of Melody when they entered, and now stood with their backs to him.

"Which one of you fellers done this?" Du Sang demanded in ugly tones. "By Gawd, I'll have——"

"He ain't here, Hugo," Manitoba put in, "he must have ducked——"

"It was Badgely's own fault," Pee-Wee was explaining heavily, at the same time. "He come here——"

"I don't care who done it!" Du Sang thundered. "The feller that plugged my foreman has gotta face me——"

He paused abruptly, noticing that the eyes of the customers kept straying to a point behind him. Du Sang whirled suddenly, one gun half out of holster. His hands shot into the air, as he saw Melody, gun in hand.

"Take it easy, mister," came Melody's cold tones. "Put that iron away *pronto*, Manitoba!"

The two men backed slowly away from the gun covering them, Melody following step by step. He moved slightly to the center of the room, alert for the first suspicious action.

"You'll back up to that bar, that's what you'll do." Melody's words were close-clipped. "You an' Manitoba—up close, where Pee-Wee can reach your guns."

Du Sang's face flamed with impotent rage. His arms came down an inch, then quickly stretched to full length again, as Melody tilted his gun-barrel.

Melody continued, "Pee-Wee, get them guns and empty 'em. Make it snappy. They can have their smoke-wagons back, when you're through."

"Touch my guns an' it's your finish, Pee-Wee," Du Sang threatened.

"Aw, hell, Hugo," Pee-Wee protested. "Show some sense. I'm bein' gunned into this, just like you."

"Go ahead, Pee-Wee," Melody said. "You're under my protection as long as you do what I tell you to do."

Pee-Wee puffed and panted, but finally managed to reach his bulk across the bar. "Hell of a job to give a fat man," he grumbled. Finally, he secured the four guns, emptied the cylinders, then replaced the weapons in their owners' holsters.

Melody holstered his own gun, now, and walked to the bar, standing a few yards distant from Du Sang and Manitoba. He eyed the pair coldly for a moment, "Don't reload until you've left here," Melody clipped his words short. "You can leave any time you like. If you come back—come a-shootin'. That's all."

Du Sang forced a smile. "I ain't leavin' yet," he said, deciding to make the best of his situation. "I want to talk to the man that done somethin' nobody else ever done—got the drop on Hugo Du Sang. You're Madigan, I'm thinkin'."

" 'Tain't necessary that you should think," Melody replied coldly. "You know damn' well Manitoba told you who I was."

Du Sang had no reply for that statement.

"Jug-Handle, hey, Jug-Handle!" Pee-Wee bellowed suddenly. "Where in the name of the seven bald steers has that hobo gone to? He was here until the shootin' started."

At that moment the tramp intruded a cautious head through the doorway at the rear of the saloon. "What you want, Pee-Wee."

"Get that carcass o'n my floor and take it to the undertaker's," was the answer, "unless——" Pee-Wee paused at a new thought and spoke to Du Sang, "Badgely was one of your outfit. What do you want done with the remains, as the paper calls 'em?"

"I don't want that body," Du Sang growled. "The undertaker's suits me. Let the county pay for buryin' the fool."

One of the customers volunteered to help, and he and Jug-Handle departed to the street with Badgely's body. A crowd, attracted by the shooting, had gathered in front of the saloon, but after Jug-Handle's explanation of the killing it quickly dispersed.

Melody turned coldly to Du Sang. "You said you wanted to talk to me. What's on your mind?"

Du Sang was anxious to appear friendly, now. "Have a drink?" he invited, and at Melody's refusal, "No? All right. What I want to know is why you rubbed out my foreman, and then stuck up me'n Manitoba?"

"That's easy," Melody replied. "I was just payin' Bull back for somethin' he handed me one time. He got the breaks before. I got 'em this time. There can't be no charge of murder lodged against me, 'cause everybody in here saw Bull's guns out, before I'd touched mine. On top of that he invited my draw. Knowin' Bull, I kinda figured he'd have friends near by. That's why I covered you, until

50

everybody had had a chance to cool down. That's all there is to it."

"But I don't understand," Du Sang frowned. "If he had his guns out, how did you beat him to the shot?"

Melody grinned. "Pure luck. I couldn't do it again in a hundred years. As a matter of fact, I ain't no gun-artist, a-tall."

Du Sang was puzzled. "I note you pack two smoke-rods," he pointed out. "That ain't done usually, unless a feller is a killer or a law-officer."

"You're packin' two yourself," Melody countered. "So's Manitoba. Badgely did, too."

"That don't mean nothin,'" from Du Sang. "We just carry two, 'cause they balance a feller's weight better."

"I carry two 'cause I want to," Melody retorted. "Any further questions?"

"You a cattle dick?" Du Sang shot at him.

Again Melody laughed. "Good Lord! If this ain't the most inquisitive town I ever see. Well, if I was one of these here deteckative hombres I wouldn't tell you any-way, so what difference does it make?"

"A lot," Du Sang answered. "Regardless of what's been said and done, I'm offerin' you a job on the Diamond-8. Good pay, too."

Melody shook his head. "You don't talk my language, Du Sang. I'm already hired to the Rafter-S."

Du Sang started. "Rafter-S!" he exclaimed. "Hell! You're just wastin' time. Norris ain't got no money for wages——"

"There's a reason for that, too," Melody said evenly. "A reason I figure to look into. To tell the truth, Norris don't know yet that I'm workin' for him, but he will tonight."

"Don't know you're workin' for him?" Du Sang was losing the drift of the conversation now.

Melody suddenly dropped his easy attitude. "Look here, Du Sang," he said sternly, "you'n me might just as well get ourselves on our correct ranges right now. Norris has got a fight on his hands, and it don't look like he's gettin' his rights."

"Why don't he appeal to the law then?" Du Sang sneered.

"From what I understand of law around here," Melody replied, "I don't think Norris has got a coyote's chance of

51

gettin' any legal justice. I always did like an underdog scrap, so I'm goin' to see if I can't help him get some gun justice. In other words, I'm out to help him down certain skunks."

"Meanin' who?" Du Sang's tones were ugly.

"Meanin'," Melody stated flatly, "the lousy buzzards that are preventin' him from gettin' food, the thievin' skunks that's runnin' off his cattle, the yellow snakes that will shoot a girl's hawss and then run when her father throws down on 'em. Is that clear?"

"I don't know what you're talkin' about, Madigan."

"That's whatever. Manitoba understands me, anyhow. He's workin' for you. Tonight, I figure to take supplies to the Rafter-S. Does *that* mean anythin' to you?"

"Not a thing to me, personal," Du Sang answered, "but I happen to know that Norris ain't popular around here. It wouldn't surprise me in the least, Madigan, if you never reached the Rafter-S. You better be sensible and take a job with me——"

Melody smiled thinly. "I happen to recognize a threat when I see one, Du Sang. In case I shouldn't reach the Rafter-S, I'm callin' on Pee-Wee, and every other man here, to remember what you've said. Law ain't quite dead, Du Sang, *but you will be*, unless you change your ways a heap."

Du Sang's face flamed with anger. "You accusin' me of pickin' on Norris?" he growled.

"Yeah, I am," Melody snapped. "I'm just sorry I ain't got proof, or we'd settle things here and now. Unless you and Manitoba got somethin' further to say, Du Sang, you might as well be driftin'. I'm through talkin' to you."

"But *I'm* not through with *you* by a damn sight!" Du Sang roared angrily. "Just remember that."

He turned and flung himself through the doorway. Manitoba hesitated just a minute, a sneering smile on his lips. "Your one best bet, Madigan," he said, "is to take that job Hugo offered. Otherwise your life won't be worth a hoot in hell."

Melody smiled. "Manitoba," he drawled softly, "if that's a warnin', I'm not needin' it. If it's a threat, what say we settle things, now?"

"It was a warnin'—nothin' else," Manitoba said hastily.

"I ain't needin' it—nor your presence, neither," Melody shot back at him. "Hit the dirt, feller."

Manitoba back slowly toward the doorway, then, reaching it, turned and stepped into the darkened street. A few yards from the saloon he found Hugo Du Sang waiting for him.

Du Sang growled, "Madigan's poison, ain't he? That's one fact we got to face. Damn Badgely for a liar! I know, now, that he never did down Madigan—leastwise, not unless he shot him in the back, or somethin' of that kind——"

"S'help me, Hugo, I couldn't do anythin'. Cripes! Madigan's gun was coverin' both of us, th' minute we stepped into the Here's A Go——"

"I ain't growlin' about your part," Du Sang grunted. "Me, I was plumb stopped, too. No use denyin it—Madigan won the first pot in this game——"

"But there'll be another deal, won't there, Hugo?" Manitoba asked anxiously.

Du Sang laughed harshly. "One more deal. That's all we're goin' to need. I'm sick of this palaverin'. *One more deal.* Remember that, Manitoba. And Du Sang will rake in all the chips."

"I'm waitin' to hear about it."

Du Sang explained, "This Madigan hombre figures to take supplies out to the Rafter-S, tonight, eh? You heard him say that?"

"Yeah, I did. But what are you——"

"Madigan ain't never goin' to reach the Rafter-S with no supplies," Du Sang swore. "C'mon, let's go down to the Silver Spur and get a drink. I got a scheme. We'll talk it over with Hump and Gus Randle. Them two's elected to show Madigan that it don't pay to buck Hugo Du Sang —show Madigan and everybody else in Vaca Wells. The four of us will make some medicine that'll stop Madigan plenty *pronto!*"

# 8. Melody Buys Supplies

THE excitement in the Here's A Go finally subsided. One by one customers departed to tell their friends of the happening. Inside half an hour Melody and Pee-Wee were left alone, Jug-Handle not yet having returned from the undertaker's.

Pee-Wee sighed deeply as the last patron of his bar stepped through the exit to the street. He said sadly, "You ain't got no relatives or wives I should break the sad news to, have you?"

"What news you referrin' to?" Melody wanted to know.

For answer, Pee-Wee gazed silently and with considerable concern in his features, at Melody. Finally, he turned to his cash till behind the bar, and removed some money. To this, he added several gold-pieces produced from his pants' pockets. This he laid on the bar and shoved in Melody's direction.

"This here," he announced dismally, "will buy some flowers for the funeral. It only comes to 'bout two hundred bucks, but it's all I can spare at present, cowpoke."

"Who's funeral you oratin' about?" Melody queried.

"The funeral of the red-headed hombre that talked so rash like to Hugo Du Sang. Howsomever, if you don't want to take that money for flowers, use it as you think best to help the Rafter-S——"

"Hey, I don't need any money. I got some——"

"What you made peelin' a few broncs on the way down here from Montany, eh? That ain't much. You take that money, Melody. I'm glad to donate that much to the cause. It's about time I come alive and acted like a man, when there's a man's work to be done. Take it, dang you! I'll have more when that's gone."

"Mebbe you're right at that, Pee-Wee," Melody said. "I am li'ble to require more cash than I got in my jeans. Much 'bliged." He took the money, counted it and put it away in his pockets. "Well, I reckon I'll drift out and get some chow."

"Either the Paris Cafe, or the Chink's restaurant can put on a fair feed," Pee-Wee suggested. "Only, if you go to the Chink's, don't forget his beef and them eggs, I mentioned."

"I ain't li'ble to—not after that *habla* you slung. Are them places close by?"

"The Chink's joint is east from here, across the street from the Silver Spur Saloon. The Paris is t'other way down the street, right next to Toby Harris' Gents' Clothin' Store. You can't miss it. But don't be takin' no shots at Toby's advertisement. You might get your breeches full of scatter-shot——"

"Advertisement?"

Pee-Wee explained: "Toby just opened up a coupla months ago. He's got eastern ideas for runnin' his business, so he brought along one of these here wax dummies, which he dressed up in a suit of clothes. He has it standin' in front of his store. 'Course, you know what the boys done to it."

"Perforated it plenty," Melody grinned.

"Shot it full of holes until it's nigh ready to fall apart. I reckon the suit of clothes is all that holds it together, and the suit is about ready to fall off. It sorta got to be the custom for everybody that passed to take a shot at that blame dummy. But Toby's stubborn. He refuses to take it in, but he hangs around the door with a shot-gun in his hand, just hopin' for some waddy to throw down on his clothing advertisement. So I warn you, no matter how invitin' that dummy looks, you keep your iron in your holster, less'n you want a skin full of pellets."

Melody shook his head. "I ain't tempted, what with other interests waitin' for my slugs. C'mon to supper with me."

"Can't, I'm on diet. Figurin' to reduce. Besides, Jug-Handle ain't here to take care of the bar. No tellin' when he'll show up. Reckon I'll have to hire me a barkeep one of these days. Long hours is wearin' me to a shadow."

"Yeah," Melody laughed, "an elephant's shadow. You must have shrunk away to a mere three hundred pounds by this time, ain't you? You look bad, Pee-Wee, with your ribs showin' through thataway, an' deep hollows in your cheeks. If your face gets much thinner, you'll be able to shave both sides of it at once——"

"None of your sarcasm, now, younker," Pee-Wee growled good-naturedly. "But I ain't foolin' when I state I'm worryin' myself skinny. Must have lost nigh onto twenty pounds, since you drifted into Vaca Wells. You sure ain't no cure for ragged nerves. Go on, get headed for your chow, before I catch me a nervous breakdown."

"Reckon I better get movin' then," Melody grinned. "If you ever bruk down, it'd take a derrick to get you on your feet again. *Adios.*"

He swung through the doorway and stepped to the plank sidewalk. Half a block from the Here's A Go he encountered Jug-Handle, returning from the undertaker's. The tramp chuckled through his grime of whiskers when he saw the cowboy.

"Still alive, eh?" he said.

"An' kickin'," Melody added.

Apropos of nothing in particular the tramp said, "Just saw Manitoba and Du Sang drivin' the Diamond-8 buckboard outta town. They looked mad."

"They don't figure to rub me out right to once, then, eh?"

Jug-Handle didn't answer the question directly. "They both rode their broncs in," he said meaningly, "and said broncs weren't tied to the wagon when it started for home."

"Meanin'," Melody mused aloud, "that their broncs has either took wings an' flew home, or were left behind for the fellers that drove the buckboard in. I'm cravin' to know. What's their names?"

"Hump Tracy and Gus Randle," said Jug-Handle. "They're in the Paris Cafe eatin' supper, now."

"Too bad about Du Sang and Manitoba," Melody said seriously. "They pro'bly sprouted saddle sores, and don't feel like forkin' leather. Randle and Tracy have been left behind to bring the horses back. And bein' that Diamond-8 chow don't suit 'em, they stay in town for supper."

"Either that," Jug-Handle replied, "or they're stayin' behind to keep an eye on anybody that might start for the Rafter-S later in the evenin'."

"I never thought of that," Melody said dryly. "Mebbe you're right, Jug-Handle. Thanks for the information. I'll remember what you said."

56

He left the tramp and sauntered on toward the Paris Cafe. Melody entered, ordered supper and glanced about the room. Only two men sat together; the other customers seemed to be alone. Melody judged the two to be Tracy and Randle. He was sure of it a few moments later, when turning suddenly, he observed the pair watching him covertly and conversing in low tones.

Melody finished his supper before Randle and Tracy and strolled back to the hitch-rack where his pony was waiting, got into the saddle and rode to the Blue Star Livery. Here, after ordering a good feed for the pony, he entered into a discussion with the proprietor regarding the renting of a buckboard and team.

Ten minutes later he drove the wagon up before the Emporium General Store, alighted from the driver's seat and after tying the horses, mounted the steps that led to the store doorway.

The Emporium was illuminated by oil lamps swung from the ceiling, and presided over by one Zachariah Hardscrapple—known to the citizens of Vaca Wells as Hard Zach. He was a gaunt, cadaverous looking individual whose face, for some reason or other, immediately reminded Melody of a rat trap.

"Just the type to starve the women and children first," Melody said to himself, as his eyes fell upon the disagreeable features of Hard Zach.

The cowboy glanced curiously about the store at three or four loungers seated on barrels and boxes, then approached Hardscrapple who stood behind the counter, a rank-smelling cigar of doubtful material held between his thin lips.

"Good evenin'," Melody greeted, stopping before the counter.

"Is it?" Hardscrapple replied sourly.

"My mistake," Melody grinned. "It was, until I come in here."

One of the loungers snickered. Hard Zach drew the cigar from his mouth, licked the wrapper, replaced it and blew a cloud of foul smoke into the air. "You wantin' something, young man?" he demanded severely. "This ain't no social parlor to talk about the weather in. This here is a general store."

"Is it?" Melody glanced meaningly at the cigar. "My mistake again," he apologized pleasantly. "I thought mebbe

57

it was a blacksmith shop. Sorta smelled like somebody was shoein' a hawss."

There came a loud guffaw from a nearby cracker barrel. "He's a-slanderin' your see-gar, Zach," a man said.

Hardscrapple's face turned a deep yellow. "This here," he announced crabbily, "is a good ten-cent smoke."

"Jesse James was more honest about such things," Melody chided gently. "Anyway, I ain't interested in your cigars right now. That one you're smokin' reminds me too much of a brand-iron at work. I want some flour."

"I've heerd about you, young man," Hard Zach stated disagreeably, making no move to fill the order. "You——"

"You're to be congratulated," Melody cut in airily. "Du Sang pro'bly advertised me as intendin' to buy a bill of goods for the Rafter-S. Yeah, I'm Melody Madigan. Now that we know each other, how about some flour?"

"Fellers that buck Du Sang," Hardscrapple announced with ominous solemnity, "don't get far as a rule."

"I never work by rule," Melody responded. "By guess or Gosh, that's me, Halfscramble. Now, regardin' that flour——"

"Ain't got none," Hardscrapple snapped, "nor nothin' else for Tom Norris!"

"No?" Melody's voice had suddenly turned chilly. "Hardscrapple, you should know your stock better. I can see your sacks of flour on that back shelf. Now, trot 'em out—two sacks—and be plenty pronto about it, regardless of what Du Sang told you to do."

A tense silence descended on the store. Melody swung half around to watch the other men in the place. Their eyes fell before his direct gaze. He turned back to the proprietor.

"Sometimes," Melody prompted softly, "when folks don't just go the way I like 'em to, I have to persuade 'em. Now, you'll notice I'm wearin' a persuader on each hip. Do I get supplies or don't I?"

"You do," Hardscrapple grunted reluctantly. He turned and shuffled to the back of the store, then returned with two sacks of flour which he dropped on the board counter.

"That's fine!" Melody was all good nature again. "Now, lemme see—oh, yes, I'll want some peaches. 'Bout half a dozen cans, an' tomatoes. Gimme a side of bacon, too. An' some Arbuckle coffee. Got any tea? Don't forget bakin' powder. Throw in some Durham and Granger's

Twist an' a coupla corncobs. I'll bet you'd like to peddle some of them sardines, wouldn't you? I wonder should I get beans. Yeah, better gimme a few—not many. An' don't overlook matches. Le's see—dried apples an' apricots is good for pies——"

For the next half hour Melody kept Hardscrapple in a streaming state of perspiration running from shelves to counter. The cowboy bought of practically everything the store had to offer. Remembering that Jerry Norris had worn overalls, he even purchased several yards from a bolt of green-and-white checked gingham which caught his eye, not forgetting to include needles and thread.

Hardscrapple paused only once in his labors, his head dropping in an almost imperceptible nod to one of the loungers. This man arose from the box upon which he'd been seated and left the store for the street. Melody caught the action, but said nothing.

By now the counter was piled high with supplies. "Mebbe," Melody smiled. "It'd been cheaper to buy your store out-right, Harshscruples."

"You're just a-wastin' your money, Madigan," Hard Zach grumbled. "Norris won't never repay——"

"Oh, yeah," Melody broke in, "I want a scatter-gun, too. Twelve gauge. An' some shells——"

"Ain't got no guns——"

"You're a liar," Melody contradicted cheerfully. "They're in that rack standin' behind the door, in case you've forgot. My gracious, Hashgrubble, you oughta do somethin' about your memory. It's terrible! Mebbe old age is creepin' on you. An' you with such a complete stock, too. You should put in a line of clothing and run Toby Harris outta business. But, shucks, I gotta hunch you ain't goin' to be in business much longer. Vaca Wells is due to get wise to you most any day, now."

Muttering oaths under his breath, Hardscrapple made his way to the gun rack. Melody followed him and picked out a double-barreled shot-gun, then his eye falling on a rifle, he picked that up and looked it over.

"This thirty-thirty Winchester looks plumb good, too," he remarked. "Better lay it on the heap, Hardscrumple. Don't forget the ca'tridges. An' it won't be a bad idea to add some forty-five slugs. Norris used some today, an' mebbe he's runnin' short. Coupla boxes."

A moment later he added, somewhat reluctantly, "I

reckon that's all, Hardsquabble. Add up the bad news, and remember I'm a poor lonesome cowboy that ain't goin' to be done wrong."

Hard Zach added the long columns of figures which he had jotted down on a scrap of paper, then told Melody the amount.

Melody sighed. " 'Member what I told you, Halfsquibbled, 'bout Jesse James bein' more honest 'bout such things? I'm repeatin' muh statement, with the reg'lar apologies to Jesse. He was a tinhorn compared to you."

"They ain't no law compellin' you to buy," Hardscrapple snarled.

"There oughta be one compellin' you to sell at an honest profit, though." Melody paid the amount asked, then, "Now, that I'm broke again, I feel more natural—— No, Hunkscribble, you don't need to help me carry these things to my wagon. I can do it."

"Nobody's offerin'," Hard Zach growled. "Carry 'em yourself. You're jest a-wastin' your time——"

" 'Cause you think they ain't never goin' to be delivered, and you figure to get 'em back, eh?" Melody grinned. "Betcha ten bucks I get 'em through."

"I ain't no bettin' man," Hardscrapple refused piously.

"Your kind generally ain't, less'n you can lay your chips on a sure thing."

It required several trips to get the supplies loaded into the wagon, but it was finally accomplished, Then, Melody mounted to the driver's seat and tooled the team down the street until he came to the Here's A Go.

Melody entered the saloon to find it had gathered several customers in his absence. It was some time before he gained an opportunity to talk with Pee-Wee. Finally, the fat proprietor waddled down to the end of the bar where the cowboy waited.

"Still figurin' on takin' supplies to the Rafter-S?" Pee-Wee queried skeptically, in a low voice.

Melody nodded, "Uh-huh. Hired a wagon and got it loaded, out front, right now. Your money come handy, Pee-Wee. I got enough goods to start a revolution in *mañana* land. Hardscrapple wa'n't eager to sell, at first, but he got to seein' things my way. Two of the Diamond-8 punchers was hangin' around town——"

"Hump Tracy an' Gus Randle," Pee-Wee interrupted. "Them two ain't pillars of no church, nuther. Plumb bad, both of 'em. Jug-Handle told me he saw 'em pull out a while back."

"That's them. Hardscrapple nodded a message to a feller that was in the store, and the feller left immediate. They didn't think I saw it, but I did. I reckon he told Tracy and Randle that I was gettin' ready to leave."

Pee-Wee sadly shook his head. "An' them two will be waitin' for you along the trail with one of their dry-gulchin' tricks. You'll never get through, son. Better wait, and I'll see can I get somebody I can trust to go along with you——"

"I'm needin' money bad, Pee-Wee," Melody said. "My bronc an' rig is in the livery. Worth a hundred, I'd say. Wanta make a bet I won't get through?"

"A horse ain't no good to me," Pee-Wee grunted seriously, "but I got bettin' in my blood. Good luck, son. I hope I lose——"

"Hey, Pee-Wee!" A voice from the opposite end of the bar. "Rattle your hocks. We're needin' service."

"S'long," Pee-Wee whispered hoarsely. He swung heavily around and shuffled back to take the orders.

Melody departed and climbed back on his wagon. He was just passing Toby Harris' Gents' Clothing Store, when he was struck by a sudden thought. He reined the horses to the side of the street and pulled to a halt. "Reckon if I'm goin' callin'," Melody chuckled, "I oughta get me some new doodad to wear."

Harris was just closing up for the night when Melody arrived at the store door. He glanced suspiciously at the cowboy, saw that Melody had made no move to harm the clothes dummy standing in front, then swung open the door.

Melody entered, and after some conversation purchased a bright green silk handkerchief which he knotted about his throat in place of his faded bandanna. Then, bidding good night to Harris, he left the store.

He paused a moment before the doorway to roll and light a cigarette. Behind him the lights were suddenly extinguished and the key turned in the lock, as Harris prepared to retire to his bed at the rear of the shop.

There weren't many people on the street, now. Melody glanced both ways along the thoroughfare. Not a horseman was in sight. To the cowboy's left stood the wax dummy with its battered face and sun-faded, bullet-riddled suit of clothes which custom prescribed as the proper raiment for the socially-inclined of Vaca Wells.

Melody grinned as his eyes fell on the dummy. "What do you think, Horatio," he chuckled, "is Randle and Tracy goin' to wait for me just outside of town, or will it be farther on? Huh? You ain't very talkative, are you? If you think they ain't waitin' for me a-tall, nod your head. H'mmm. You think they are, eh? You're pro'bly correct as hell. What'll I do about it? All right, if you don't want to commit yourself, don't speak, then."

He dropped his cigarette butt, smothered it with one toe, and exhaled twin plumes of gray smoke. "Well, if I reckon to reach the Rafter-S tonight, I oughta be startin'. Time, tide an' Melody Madigan waits for no man. We'll see what sort of lead Randle an' Tracy can throw."

# PART III

# *Ambush!*

## 9.

TWO MEN huddled in the brush on either side of a small hollow that marked the approach to the Rafter-S valley. There was no moon, and the stars gave only a faint light that reflected dully on their belt buckles when they moved a trifle, now and then.

"Dammit, Hump!" Gus Randle said, low-voiced, "if that hombre is really figurin' to come through tonight, I certain wish he'd hurry."

"Mebbe he won't come," Hump Tracy suggested.

"Hard Zach sent word that Madigan was orderin' a heap of supplies, didn't he? And didn't Madigan tell Hugo right to his face that he was goin' to bring some groceries to the Rafter-S——"

"I mean, mebbe he'll wait until tomorrow."

"Oh, I get you. I'm hopin' not. I'd like to get this business over an' done with. Don't see why Hugo and Manitoba didn't handle it theirselves."

"What do you care?" Tracy asked. "We're drawin' a nice bonus if we rub out Madigan."

Randle gulped uneasily. "Yeah, and if somethin' should go wrong, you know what it means. Hugo said *he'd* drill us—if Madigan didn't."

"What could go wrong?"

"I dunno—only somethin' might. Suppose Madigan should hear our broncs, or somethin', and circle around us?"

"Hell! Feller, don't be so skeery. Them hawsses is staked out far enough back. He won't hear 'em. You needn't worry. We got everythin' our way. All we gotta do is fill Madigan full of lead when he drives that wagon past."

The two men fell silent. It was well after midnight by this time. Madigan should arrive before long. Suddenly,

Hump Tracy sat up, one hand cupped about his ear. "Think I hear him," he announced.

Gus Randle also listened, then nodded. "Team and wagon comin', all right. It must be Madigan."

The two men drew their Colt-guns and moved a trifle closer to the wagon-rutted road that lay but a few yards away. From some distance down the trail came the squeak of wheels, pounding of hoofs, and rattle of harness trappings. The sounds came nearer. Hump and Randle could hear Melody singing:

> Sam Bass had a gal up Frisco way;
> To him she would be wed,
> But an outlaw's life is full of strife,
> And so to her he said:

The song broke off a minute while Melody spoke to the horses. The noises of the team and wagon became more distinct. Again, Melody lifted his voice to explain Sam Bass' excuse for not entering into a holy state of matrimony:

> A widow you might sudden be
> If I took a lovin' wife;
> So do not cry, but say good-bye;
> I'm ridin' out of your life.

"That bird ain't no canary," Hump Tracy muttered. "If he didn't shoot no better than he warbles, Badgely would still be alive."

"Damn' red-headed fool," from Randle. "He ain't even makin' an attempt to sneak along. Must be he don't realize that Hugo Du Sang won't stand no monkeyin'. We'll get a good look at him, just before he drives down through this hollow. When he gets abreast of us, let him have it."

The two men crouched closer in the shielding brush. Melody drew nearer, now. It seemed that the girl's father objected to Sam Bass' plans:

> But then her paw he says to Sam:
> Young man, you'd best stay here;
> With this shot-gun, I'll make you one;
> So Sam lived another year-r-r.

As the last long-drawn notes of the song left the singer's

mouth, the team and wagon appeared at the rim of the hollow. The two would-be killers could see, dimly silhouetted against the starry sky, the wagon piled high with supplies, and the figure slouched on the driver's seat.

"Take it easy, now, you pair of spavined crowbaits," they heard Melody mutter, as the team dipped down the descent. "I'll skin your hides if you tip me over."

The wagon came nearer, as the crouching Randle and Tracy lifted their forty-fives. It was almost abreast of them.

"Let him have it!" Tracy said hoarsely.

The night was suddenly shattered with a series of savage reports, the gloom slashed with bright streaks of orange fire! The figure on the driver's seat swayed to one side, then toppled from the wagon. Startled by the explosions, the horses reared and scrambled wildly, their frightened hoofs digging frantically into the turf.

Randle and Tracy leaped from their place of concealment. "We got him!" Tracy yelled triumphantly. He ran to the head of the team and brought the horses to a halt. "Keep an eye on Madigan, Gus!"

"I'll do more than keep an eye on him," Randle grated savagely. "I'll make sure." He was standing over the prostrate figure on the ground, now, and leveling his gun at its head, he proceeded to empty his cylinder.

"That was a right idea," Tracy exclaimed, as he came running back from the team. "Nothin' like makin' sure, Gus——"

"Wait a minute." Randle's tones were queer. In the light from the gun flashes he thought he had noticed something odd. "Light a match, Hump."

There came a moment's silence. Then a scratching sound, and a match flared in Tracy's hand. But they didn't have time to examine the object of their murderous slugs.

"I'm afeared you've slayed Horatio," came a voice of assumed grief from the direction of the wagon.

Randle and Tracy whirled, mouths hanging open in dumb amazement. Tracy still held the lighted match. In the midst of the piled supplies sat Melody Madigan, a leveled gun in each hand.

"Drop your smoke-rods, skunks," Melody snapped. "Then unbuckle your belts and let 'em drop to the ground. Hurry! I'm sure cravin' to unravel some lead at you buzzards!"

The match flickered out in Tracy's hand, but Melody

caught the sounds of the guns as they struck the earth. A few seconds later, belts were unbuckled, and also allowed to drop. Melody laughed softly as he eyed the two men, their hands high in the air.

"Where—where was you?" Tracy stammered, at last.

"Layin' in the wagon, of course," Melody chuckled. "Hidden under the supplies. This ought to be a lesson to you fellers, not to believe everythin' you see. Yo're shore dumb, but you put me to a heap of trouble, at that. I kinda figured you'd lay for me in this hollow, seein' it's the most likely place for an ambushin', so I stole Toby Harris' clothes dummy, and fixed it on the driver's seat——"

Randle broke out in a fit of cursing.

"Yep." Melody went on, "that dummy sure come in handy. I named him Horatio, thinkin' he might get friendly, but he ain't sociable, nohow. I ought to complain to Toby. Why, Horatio wouldn't talk, or help me drive, or nothin'. Just sat there, dumb like, and I had to hold him up with one hand and drive with the other. It ain't no cinch to drive a team with the lines passed under the seat. An' you thought you was shootin' at me, huh? Ain't that funny? Two dummies slingin' lead at a dummy. I bet Du Sang will laugh most fit to bust when he hears how you two brought about Horatio's untimely demise—yes he will, *not!*"

"Well, what you goin' to do about it," Randle said sullenly. "Me'n Hump ain't——"

Hump Tracy broke in, whining, "It was Du Sang put us up to this, Madigan. He made us do it. We didn't want to, but he——"

"What I got a good notion to do," Melody announced, his voice suddenly icy, "is fill you both full of lead and send the bodies to the Diamond-8. But I ain't no murderer. I'll give you a chance. Clear outta the country and stay out, and I won't stop you. If you want to stay and listen to Vaca Wells hooraw you about wastin' lead on a wax figure, that's your problem, but I'm warnin' you—I'll shoot on sight, next time you cut my trail. Make your choice—quick!"

"We'll be travelin'," Randle replied in harsh, strained tones. "We wouldn't dare face Du Sang, after this——"

"Get goin' then," Melody snapped, "an' don't stop to pick any violets along the way."

"We want our guns—" Tracy commenced.

"So do I. Get goin'!" Melody's voice was stern.

There was no further conversation. The two would-be bad-men turned and made their way up to the rim of the hollow. For just a brief instant, Melody saw their forms blocked against the sky, then they disappeared from sight.

Guns still in hand, not quite trusting the two, he sat waiting on the wagon. Fifteen minutes passed, then, off to his left, he heard the staccato pounding of running hoofs. Melody chuckled. "They're driftin', all right. Headin' north. Well, that's as it should be."

He threw his legs over the side of the wagon and dropped to earth. A few minutes' search located the belts and guns of the two Diamond-8 men. He tossed them in with the supplies. Then he picked up the bullet-riddled clothes dummy. "Poor Horatio, I knew him well," Melody laughed, as he lifted the wax figure to the top of the heap. A few moments later he climbed to the driver's seat, spoke to the horses and moved off down the valley.

Some time within the next half hour Melody neared the house. As he had expected, it was dark. What he didn't expect was the sudden flash of fire from one of the windows, and the rifle bullet that winged viciously past his head!

Melody yanked the team to haunches with astounding speed, made haste to leap to the ground and crouch down behind the horses.

"I've warned you hombres to stay away from here," came the wrathy tones of Tom Norris, "and I meant every word I said. Now vamose!"

"Hey, hold that fire, Norris," Melody yelled. "I ain't no Diamond-8 man. This is me—Melody Madigan."

An instant's silence. Then Melody caught the girl's voice. "It's that fellow who loaned me his horse—the one that thinks he's a singer. He's harmless."

Melody's ears burned. He checked the retort that rose to his lips, and again called, "Well, do I get in, or don't I?"

Tom Norris again, something hostile in the tones, "What do you want?"

"I'm your new foreman, and I'm bringing that load of grub and other stuff you need."

He heard a whispered conversation taking place at the window, the girl's low voice: "He's crazy as a bat. Maybe we better let him in and see what he wants." Then Norris replied, "Keep that rifle ready. I'll take the Colt and go see." He raised his voice a moment later. "I'll be right out, Madigan."

A minute passed. A light sprung into being in the house. The door opened, and Norris emerged, hobbling with the aid of a cane improvised from the leg of a table. In his other hand he carried his forty-five, ready for instant use. "Now what's all this foolishness?" he demanded tartly.

"Mebbe it is, at that," Melody agreed sheepishly, rising from his position behind the horses, "only from what I've heard, I kinda thought you might need some help—a foreman, anyway. So I started my job by bringing you some grub."

By this time Norris had seen the loaded wagon. "Well, I'll be damned!" he gasped weakly. "I don't understand. It's a wonder Du Sang didn't try to prevent you coming here." He lowered his six-gun. "What's the idee, anyhow——"

"I've told you," Melody answered. "I'm takin' sides with you, just to make Du Sang peeved. Now, do we unload this wagon, or don't we?"

"If there's food there, by all means unload it!" came Jerry Norris' fervent voice. She came hurrying from the house, carrying the Winchester. "I reckon I misjudged you, cowboy. I'm not understandin' any more than Dad does, but it comes to me that there's another real man besides Tom Norris in this country. Dad, you go in the house. I'll help Melody with the supplies."

Somewhat bewildered by the turn events had taken, Norris reëntered the house and Melody and Jerry commenced sorting out the packages and cans. The girl gave a little squeal of fright upon discovering the clothes dummy.

"Don't be skeered," Melody chuckled. "Horatio won't hurt you. I lifted him in front of Toby Harris' store, but he got killed on the way here. Put him on the driver's seat and loaned him my Stet hat, and a coupla hombres mistook him for me and slung lead at him——"

"Melody! You did have trouble!"

"Aw, none to speak of. Mostly, it was just fun. I'll tell you about it, later. Let's get this wagon emptied first."

# 10. "We'll Be Needin' Help"

EVERYTHING was finally carried inside the ranch-house. The goods overflowed the kitchen table and chairs upon which they were placed. Jerry uttered little cries of delight as she examined the various packages. Finally, "Checked gingham! Melody! How in the world did you ever happen to buy this?"

Involuntarily he glanced at her overalls, then noticing her flushed cheeks, he turned away. "Oh, I dunno," he mumbled. "Thought mebbe you could use it for window curtains, or bed-sheets, or table-cloths, or somethin'."

"I'll probably use it for *somethin'*," she giggled. She continued her inspection of cans and sacks. "Coffee! You don't know how long it is since we've had any of that! I'm goin' to make some, right now."

Cheeks flushed with happiness, tousled red hair clinging in tiny tendrils about her face, the girl hurried to the stove and put on the coffee pot, after starting a fire Melody settled to a chair in the big kitchen, watching her.

Tom Norris sat across the room, still lost in a daze at the unlooked-for good fortune. "I reckon," he said at last in an awkward voice of apology, "that I'm sorry I slung that thuty-thuty slug at you, Madigan. I dang near made a fool of myself."

"And an angel of me," Melody grinned. "You can save your slugs for the Du Sang crowd, from now on. I brought you another rifle and a shot-gun. Picked up a coupla Colt-guns on the way here, too."

Norris was a loose-limbed man with a weathered face and honest blue eyes, which at present were a trifle moist. He rose and crossed the floor to Melody. Words wouldn't come, but there was considerable warmth in the grip he gave the cowboy.

Crackers were opened, and sardines and peaches. Jerry poured the coffee, and the three sat down. Melody felt a

69

lump come into his throat as he watched Jerry and her father consume food. They were a long way from starvation, but pretty hungry just the same.

Norris' explanation was apologetic: "I killed a cow and took it to town and sold it for a few dollars, but Hardscrapple wouldn't sell me no supplies. Me'n Jerry got sorta tired of eatin' beef all the time, and these vittles just touch the spot."

"From now on," Melody said, a trace of grimness in his tones, "you ain't goin' to have no trouble gettin' what you want. An', by the way, when you get a chance, you owe Pee-Wee Page some thanks. He kicked in two hundred for this load of chow———"

"Page!" Norris exclaimed. "Why, I thought———"

"You thought you didn't have no friends in this country," Melody cut in, "but you're goin' to learn different. I'm offerin' my services as a foreman to begin with— wait! I know you ain't got no money for wages, but we won't talk about that. I decided to throw in with you when I first saw Jerry today, and I ain't been idle since."

From that point on, Melody told everything that had happened to him from the moment he arrived at Vaca Wells, including the fight with Badgely, the meeting with Du Sang and the encounter with Tracy and Randle on the way to the Rafter-S. Jerry's eyes were shining frank admiration by the time he had finished.

"Haven't I been telling you, Dad," she said, "that it wouldn't help any to worry? Put your trust in the ravens, they'll feed you every time—'specially red-headed ravens." She drained her coffee cup with a long sigh of contentment, and commenced rolling cigarettes for the two men, while they discussed the situation.

"Yes," Norris said at last, "Page gave you pretty much all the information there was to give. We haven't any proof, of course, but it's Du Sang doin' the rustlin' around here. He wants my place, because the water on his own holdin's is peterin' out. We've been here about six years. Du Sang come in a mite over three years ago.
The first year he come, everybody lost a few cows, but the last two years he's been makin' me the heavy loser———"

"Page said somethin' about that," Melody broke in. "He told me Du Sang tried to buy the Rafter-S from you."

Norris nodded. "Yes, coupla years back—but he only offered about a fifth of what it's worth———. When Jerry's ma died. we sold our old place up no'th, and come down here. At the time I took over the Rafter-S it was mortgaged to the hilt, but I worked hard, and we was gettin' it paid off in fine shape. After my cows commenced disappearin', though, I couldn't make any money. Had to let all my help go. To top that off, Du Sang took over the mortgage on this place, and he's doin' his best to keep me from makin' my final payments."

"Pee-Wee didn't tell me about that," Melody said. "Mebbe he didn't know Du Sang held the mortgage on the Rafter-S."

"Pro'bly hadn't heard of it," Norris replied. "To the best of my knowledge, Du Sang never registered that mortgage. Some time back he figured to put me out of the way, altogether. One of his gunmen met me in Vaca Wells and started a fight. I beat him to the draw and wiped him out, but he succeeded in throwin' a slug into my laig an' broke it. That's held me back a heap, too. Otherwise, I'd have gone some place else for my supplies, and I didn't want to take a chance on Jerry makin' a long trip alone."

"Dad thinks I can't take care of myself," Jerry put in scornfully.

"I don't blame him," Melody replied, "so long as the Du Sangs are runnin' hawg-wild on the range. I reckon Du Sang and his gang are due for a fight right soon. I'm goin' to see what can be done about gettin' in some more help, and we'll try and put the Rafter-S on a workin' basis, again. That is, providin' I get that job I applied for."

"Job, hell!" Norris exploded. "You do everythin' you expect to do, son, and you'll come in for a share of the outfit. I figgered it as lost, anyhow. You can have anythin' the place has to offer."

"Anythin'?" Melody looked at the girl, then grinned at Norris.

Norris missed Melody's allusion, and the girl's crimson face. "Anythin'," he repeated. "Why, goldarn it, son, you've sorta give me new life already, with just thinkin' what you've done so far. Puttin' Badgely outta the way was a good move. He was bad."

They talked an hour or so longer before Melody pushed back his chair and arose. "Well, I'll be gettin' back to town. It'll be well past sun-up now, before I hit Vaca Wells, and I wanta put Horatio back in front of Toby Harris' place

71

before Harris finds out who took him. I'll drift out here again just as soon as I can."

"I was hoping you'd stay the night," Jerry invited. "We've an extra bed, and I'd like to show you I can build a real breakfast, when I've got something to work with."

"Better stay, Melody," Norris urged. "It'll be a reg'lar banquet by the time Jerry gets finished with that bunch of chow——"

"Did you bring your accordion?" Jerry broke in suddenly.

"Nope," Melody laughed. "Left it at the livery with my hawss and rig. Thought you didn't like my voice."

"Cowboy," the girl said warmly, "I'm commencin' to think you got just about the peachiest voice I've heard in a month of blue moons. I was all wrong before. When you open your mouth, you say something!"

Melody grinned widely. "Sa-a-ay, you ain't heard nothin' yet! Ain't I told you us red-heads has got to stick together? I meant it!" And having dared so much, he suddenly became covered with confusion. "All right, I'll stay the night, and get an early start tomorrow." He added, to cover his embarrassment, "Reckon I better go put them hawsses up——"

At that moment there came the sounds of running hoofs approaching the house. The two men started for the door, guns in hands.

"Better let me go," Melody said swiftly. "You stay——"

"Hello the house!" came a hail from the rider. "Is Madigan there?"

"It's Jug-Handle—that hobo that hangs around the Here's A Go," Melody said. He flung open the door and stepped outside, to find the tramp pulling to a halt.

"H'lo, Jug-Handle," the cowboy greeted, "what you wantin'?"

Jug-Handle laughed, without dismounting. "Pee-Wee just lost five bucks. I bet my week's salary you'd get through."

"He'll be owin' me a hundred, too," Melody laughed.

"He was afraid he might win," Jug-Handle explained, "so he give me that rusty o' hawglaig of his, got your hawss outta the livery, and sent me on to help, if needful. So here I am. How many of the Du Sang crowd did you have to kill to get here?"

Melody told the story. While he was talking, Norris and

Jerry came out and joined them, the girl bearing a cup of hot coffee which Jug-Handle drank with evident relish.

"I'm glad you come out, Jug-Handle," Melody said after a time. "I'll be stayin' the night, here. You can leave my hawss, and take the wagon back for me, if you will. Likewise, leave Horatio in his accustomed position, outside the Gents' Clothing Store."

"I'll do that, cowboy," Jug-Handle replied. "And tomorrow I'll do plenty tellin' of the story, too. Du Sang will be fit to be tied. Mebbe we'll be able to laugh him outta the country. Ridicule will accomplish what fightin' won't, sometimes."

He swung easily down from the pony's back and climbed to the seat of the wagon. A minute later he had doffed his tattered sombrero to Jerry, and rattled off down the valley.

Melody was thoughtful as he led his horse down to the barn, Norris and Jerry on either side of him. "Notice how that 'bo lighted from my bronc?" he asked.

"Easy like," Jerry said. Norris nodded.

"Easy is right," Melody continued. "Jug-Handle may be a tramp now, but I'm bettin' a stack of blues that he knows how to rope an' shoot, as well as ride. Cow country stuff, I calls him."

"Meanin'," Norris suggested, "that he ain't so much a tramp as he appears to be?"

"That exactly," Melody replied. "When I get back to Vaca Wells, I aim to *habla* with that hombre a mite. Mebbe we could hire him to make a hand on the Rafter-S."

"Lord knows," Norris sighed, "we'll be needin' plenty help."

# 11. Jug-Handle Talks

THE SUN was high overhead by the time Melody loped Jezebel along the main street of Vaca Wells. He had half expected to meet Du Sang or others of the Diamond-8 outfit on his return to town, but nothing of the sort had happened. He noticed several pedestrians smile and nod at him as he passed. "Folks seem to be gettin' right friendly, all of a sudden," he mused. "What's the idea, I wonder?"

As he was passing the Gents' Clothing Store, a sudden hail reached his ears. Melody shifted in the saddle and saw the chubby form of Toby Harris standing in the doorway. Melody glanced guiltily at the dummy which, looking much the worse for wear, was standing in its accustomed place.

"I want that you should talk to me," Harris called a second time.

No way out of it, it seemed. Melody reined Jezebel around and guided the little mare to the sidewalk. "You wa'n't meanin' me, was you?" Melody asked innocently.

"You're Mister Madigan, ain't it?" Harris demanded heavily. "And you took my adver-dise-ment away last night, when you left my shop."

"Guilty," Melody reluctantly admitted the charge. "What do I owe you?"

Harris came closer, mouth expanding in a sudden smile of friendliness. "Not one cent, young feller. To my clothes-figure you are welgome, any dime. These here now Du Sangs has been needin' their take downs for a long while. Dem it was what first shoot bullets at my adver-dise-ment. I am bleased that you blay a joge on dem. Dat is all."

"Thanks, Mister Harris. I won't forget," Melody shook hands with the little man, and loped off down the street.

There was quite a crowd in the Here's A Go when Melody entered the saloon—more than was usually found there at that hour of the day. Pee-Wee's eyes lighted with pleasure as they fell on the cowboy. "Back, eh, Melody," he greeted. "Glad to see you. Gents, have a drink on the house, and show Madigan we ain't all dummies when it comes to appreciatin' a joke."

There was some laughter. Many of the men glanced with open admiration at Melody as they moved up to the bar. Somewhat mystified, Melody joined them in the drink, then asked Pee-Wee, "Where's Jug-Handle?"

"Out back, loafin', I reckon," Page answered.

Melody started for the door. Pee-Wee came around the bar and joined him at the entrance. "Son, I was sure glad you put it across—even if it does cost me a hundred. I'll pay that shortly, at the rate trade is pickin' up."

"I don't quite get you," Melody frowned. "I been receivin' smiles from strangers ever since I hit town."

"It's that trick you played on Randle and Tracy. Jug-Handle has spread the story high, wide and handsome. Fellers has been driftin' in here, right along, just to hear me tell about it. Cowboy, you're the talk of Vaca Wells, and Du Sang is madder than a wet hornet."

"You better not talk too much, Pee-Wee," Melody warned. "Du Sang will be hoppin' down on you——"

"Du Sang be damned!" Pee-Wee exclaimed. "Now that you've bucked his game, they's a heap of folks are commencin' to talk openly against him. He was in here about an hour ago. His two brothers are with him. They've threatened to get me, so it doesn't matter what I say, now. They're out to get you, too. Big-Foot Higley—he's sheriff, you know—has been lookin' for you. He's just a big bluff, though. One of Du Sang's pups, of course."

"If they want me, they'll have to move pronto," Melody said grimly. "I'll be ridin' out to them other outfits you told me about, the Slash-O and Lazy-V, in a little while." He told Pee-Wee what had happened the night before, then finished, "I'm figurin' to get some help from them two outfits, if possible, but I want to see Jug-Handle first."

"He's around here some place," Pee-Wee answered. "Look for the most likely sleepin' spot, and you'll find Jug-Handle. I don't quite figure that hombre. Sometimes, I think he's just a lousy hobo. At others, I get to thinkin' about him, and I wonder if he ain't somethin' more. He's damn sharp on occasion,—when he ain't dumber than swill water. He's got me sort of stopped."

"He's got me wonderin', too," Melody admitted.

"How do you figure him?"

Melody shrugged lean shoulders. "I ain't got to that point, yet, Slim. I do know this—I've seen it in his actions —if he hasn't been one damn good cow-hand at some time or other in his life, I'm willin' to eat my Stet hat."

Pee-Wee looked dubious. "That's hard to imagine."

"I know it is," Melody agreed. "To look at him, you'd think he was just an ordinary vag, handout-moocher, bum —give it any name you like. But I ain't forgettin' it was this same Jug-Handle that brought my mare out to the Rafter-S last night——"

"Well——?"

"Jezebel," Melody explained, "don't take kindly to strangers. She's mean to sit, if a rider don't handle her just so. I know that mare, and I know dang well if Jug-Handle hadn't been a rider from hell to breakfast, the horse would never have carried him out to Norris' place."

"Mebbe there's somethin' in what you say," Pee-Wee nodded. He changed the subject. "Melody, don't you get careless, now——"

"How you meanin'?"

"Keep your eyes peeled when you step into the street. Don't let nobody get behind you. Sit with your back to a wall, when you sit. You got the Du Sang outfit on the prod with your doin's. They won't be overlookin' any opportunities to throw down on you. You got a fight ahead of you, son."

"It can't come none too soon—" Melody commenced.

"I know how you feel, cowboy, and I wish I could make a hand with you, but I'm just warnin' you to walk circumspect. When the break comes, it won't be like fightin' no ordinary gunman, where you'll get an even break. Them Du Sangs will take advantage of you in any way that offers. Them sidewinders don't know what clean fightin' is. You'll have to be on your guard, every minute."

"I reckon," Melody nodded. "Thanks, Pee-Wee——"

"No thanks due, son. I'm just tellin' you. . . . We'll talk some more when I got more time. Customers sort of keepin' me rushed, today."

He made his way back to the bar, to administer to the requirements of thirsty patrons. Melody stepped into the street and, mindful of Pee-Wee's warning words, glanced both ways along the thoroughfare. There was nothing hos-

76

tile in the actions of any of the pedestrians in sight. Nothing was to be seen of Hugo Du Sang or Manitoba.

Melody sauntered around to the rear of the saloon. Here, as Pee-Wee had prophesied, he found Jug-Handle. The tramp was seated on the ground in the shadow of the building, his back against the back wall. Snores issued at regular intervals from his open mouth.

Melody stood gazing down at the tattered figure with some amusement, then spoke softly, "That's a right good imitation of a locomotive pullin' up grade, Jug-Handle, but you can quit, now. It's only me."

Jug-Handle opened one eye and glanced up. "Howdy, Melody." The other eye opened, and he smiled lazily, "Just catchin' up on my sleep quota."

"Catchin' up?" Melody snorted. "Hell! Feller, you done passed it, some time back—if you was really sleepin'."

"Any reason why I shouldn't be sleepin——"

"There's pro'bly plenty reasons. I'm tryin' to figure which one applies to you. You're always layin' around——"

"A feller can learn things layin' around," the tramp said carelessly, "an' listenin'."

"Exactly what I wanted to see you about," Melody replied. He dropped down beside the hobo, bracing his back against a nearby whisky-barrel which had long since been emptied of its contents.

"Jug-Handle," Melody continued, "just what do you know about this range, anyway?"

"How you figurin' I know anythin'?" the tramp evaded. "I only been here a week."

Melody repeated Jug-Handle's words, "A feller can learn things, layin' around and listenin'."

Jug-Handle didn't answer for a moment. Watching him narrowly, Melody saw the dull look leave his eyes, as the tramp sat gazing off into space as though trying to decide whether or not to tell what he knew. Finally, he gave a long sigh and picked up a small stick of wood from the ground.

"It might be a good idea," he commenced, "to sketch some cattle brands for you to ponder over."

With quick, deft strokes, he traced in the sandy earth the Rafter-S brand, an inverted V-like character, with beneath it, a letter S; next came the Lazy-V, a letter V lying on its side; the third drawing represented the Slash-

O, an oblique line, with below it, a trifle to the right, a letter O.

Rafter-S       Lazy-V       Slash-O

"There's three of the brands for this neck of the range," Jug-Handle commented carelessly.

Melody studied the drawings, then raised his eyes to Jug-Handle's. Neither spoke for several moments. Finally, Melody said, "The Du Sang crowd has been here about three years, I understand."

"So I've heard."

Melody went on, "I've got a hunch that Du Sang changed his brand when he bought the present Diamond-8."

"I've heard somethin' of the kind, too," the tramp admitted.

"What exactly?" Melody asked.

"Before Du Sang got the outfit," Jug-Handle answered, "it was known as the Circle-Bar-Circle. Some called it the Bridle-Bit. Du Sang changed his iron to Diamond-8, as soon as he bought the ranch."

Melody nodded comprehension. "The evidence piles up," he drawled. He scrutinized the three brand drawings Jug-Handle had made in the earth, then took the small stick from the tramp's fingers.

"You figurin' to show me somethin'?" Jug-Handle smiled thinly.

Melody grinned suddenly, "Dang your measly hide, you already know——"

"Know what?" noncommittally.

"Oh, shucks, you know what I'm talkin' about. Look here——" Melody broke off, and sketched with the stick quick, sure additional lines that converted the three drawings Jug-Handle had made, into Diamond-8 symbols:

Melody glanced up, studied Jug-Handle's eyes. The two men exchanged understanding smiles. With one foot, Melody scuffed out all evidence of the drawings.

Diamond-8 brands converted from the Rafter-S,
Lazy-V, and Slash-O designs.

"So much explained," he commented, "I suppose it's
just coincidence that all four outfits brand on the left ribs."

"Before Du Sang got his outfit," Jug-Handle pointed
out, "that ranch used to burn the right flank. Du Sang
changed that, when he changed his iron to Diamond-8.
Sort of made it unanimous with these other three outfits."

"Unanimous is right," Melody said grimly. "If Du Sang
ever got started, he'd make a killin'. Once such brand-
blottin' had healed and haired-over it'd be mighty hard to
—wait, I haven't got the ear-markings straightened out,
yet. How do they work in?"

"It all dovetails, cowboy. Du Sang planned mighty
shrewd. The Rafter-S splits the right ear and gotches the
left. The Lazy-V swallow-forks right and left, and the
Slash-O under-half-crops both ears."

Melody frowned. "That don't leave nothin' for Du Sang
to do, but gotch—" he commenced.

"The Diamond-8," Jug-Handle finished for him,
"gotches right and left, which same cuts off all traces of
the markin's of the other three outfits."

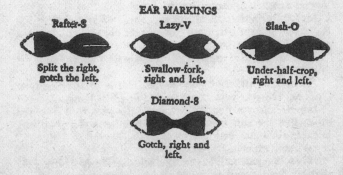

EAR MARKINGS

Rafter-S — Split the right, gotch the left.

Lazy-V — Swallow-fork, right and left.

Slash-O — Under-half-crop, right and left.

Diamond-8 — Gotch, right and left.

"Devilish neat, I calls it," Melody commented admiringly. "Wonder folks haven't noticed this before, though."

"Folks is plumb trustful, sometimes. At beef round-up, the Lazy-V and Slash-O have always worked together, coverin' the territory that lays east of Vaca Wells. The Diamond-8 and Rafter-S are supposed to take care of the range west of town. Norris' round-up has been limited the last couple of years, and there wa'n't nobody in particular to check up the Diamond-8 activities. 'Nother thing, Du Sang never ships with the other spreads, but drives his stock down below the Mexican Border. He claims to have a regular market down there."

"I don't doubt that none. He'd have a market for stolen beef, and he wouldn't dare run the chance of selling it this side of the line. Probably got regular customers down in *mañana* land for all the rustled stock he'll drive down there. Jug-Handle, this range has been too damn careless——"

"Admitted. You got any particular type of carelessness in mind?"

Melody nodded. "Du Sang is dang clever, fixin' things so he can take care of brands and ear-marks both. But we can stop him with the use of stamp-irons."

"That's an idea, cowbody."

"You're right, it is. It's time runnin' irons went out of use on this range. Nowdays, nigh everybody uses stamp-irons. Folks around here has been just too lazy to make the change, or didn't want to go to that expense. . . . Jug-Handle, did you ever consider goin' to work?"

"Who, me?" The tramp's mouth dropped open, he looked shocked at the very thought.

Melody grinned. "Step out of character and act natural for a few minutes. I got a hunch you got the makin' of a good hand——"

"You'd have a tough time convincin' Vaca Wells of that."

"I'm not considerin' Vaca Wells. This is between us two. I asked, did you ever consider indulgin' in honest labor?"

Jug-Handle yawned. "*Considered* it—yes. Two or three times I've thought of takin' jobs—had 'em offered to me, in fact. But I always turned 'em down."

"What happened? Why?"

"Well, you see," the tramp said seriously, "any jobs that I got interested in, always had some sort of work connected with 'em, so I plumb relinquished the thought. Nope——" he mournfully shook his head, "——work ain't for me."

"You're a liar," Melody grinned genial contradiction. "Feller, I ain't so green as I am cabbage-lookin', but we'll go into certain things later. First, I want to high-tail it out to the Slash-O and Lazy-V, and see can I drum up some hands for Norris. You're hired, now, of course——"

"Aw, Melody," Jug-Handle pleaded, "my constitution won't stand up under hard work——"

"You're hired right now," Melody said firmly. "I don't want no arguments. Your first job is to drop over to the blacksmith shop and order some Rafter-S stamp-irons made up. It won't take long. Then, get out to Norris' place and tell him I put you on——"

"But, Melody, I don't want——"

"But me no buts. If you talk back I might fire you. If I do that, you're goin' to miss one fine shindig. . . . You tell Norris I want all the country combed around his valley. I've got a hunch there's more cows there than Norris thinks he's got. Norris mebbe can't ride yet, but that'll be somethin' for you to start on. We'll have more help later. Thank God, the Rafter-S has got some ponies left, anyhow——"

# 12. Cornered!

MELODY broke off suddenly. Both men tensed, then swiftly gained their feet. Stealthy sounds from around the corner of the building had reached their ears. Rounding the edge of the structure, Melody saw Hugo Du Sang and two other men, moving hastily away.

"Wa'n't lookin' for me, was you, Du Sang?" Melody queried softly.

Du Sang and his two companions whirled like a flash. Melody, after the first glance, guessed that the other two were Du Sang's brothers, Guy and Luke. But the resemblance ended with their features. Guy was slender, with a wisp of a mustache adorning his upper lip. He appeared to be something of a dandy, considering the robin's-egg blue silk shirt and beaded throat-latch on his Stetson.

Luke was Guy's direct antithesis—slovenly, bristly jowls, stoop-shouldered. His long limbs were clad in dirty overalls, and his mud-colored hair hung down before his small, pig-like eyes. However, the guns of both brothers looked efficient.

Du Sang didn't answer Melody's question at once. His face reddened a trifle, then, "No, Madigan, I ain't lookin' for you—yet. But Sheriff Higley is."

"You can tell the sheriff I've been around quite a while," Melody replied coolly. "Furthermore, I'm aimin' to stay a considerable spell longer."

"Don't be too sure of that, Madigan—" Luke Du Sang commenced.

"You let me handle this, Luke," Hugo cut in angrily. He again directed his attention to Melody. "Madigan, folks don't buck me and get away with it."

"No?" Melody laughed scornfully. "I bucked a coupla your crew last night, Du Sang—made monkeys of 'em, in fact. In case you're wonderin' what's become of Randle and Tracy, they're high-tailin' it out of the country as fast as they can go—on my orders!"

Hugo Du Sang flushed. "I don't care nothin' about them. Didn't even know they intended holdin' you up——"

"Expect me to believe that?" Melody drawled.

"Don't give a damn whether you do or not," Du Sang growled. "Just remember, I ain't through with you yet, Madigan. Come on, boys." He wheeled abruptly, and followed by Luke, stepped back to the street and disappeared around the corner of the Here's A Go.

Guy Du Sang lingered a moment, a sarcastic smile playing about his lips. "Madigan," he said softly, a smooth purring quality in the tones, "Hugo said he wasn't through with you yet. I haven't even started with you. When I do, look out!"

"That's fine, Handsome," Melody smiled, but his eyes were cold. "In case you feel the urge to start, now, fill your hand."

Guy Du Sang slowly shook his head, held his hands well away from gun-butts. "The time ain't come yet, Madigan—but it will." Then, he, too, turned and was gone.

"So them's the three Du Sang brothers, eh?" Melody said to Jug-Handle a minute later. "That youngest one is a snaky sort of critter, ain't he? I kinda underestimated him at first, due to his dude appearance, but I reckon he's as deadly a sidewinder as a man would want to find in his blankets."

"Amen to that, brother," Jug-Handle said solemnly. "I wonder if they heard much of what we was sayin'."

Melody shrugged his shoulders. "It don't much matter, I reckon. We're both old enough to keep our eyes open, anyway. Jug-Handle, when you ride to the Rafter-S you better take that Colt-gun of Pee-Wee's with you. It ain't no great shucks as a weapon, but it might come handy. Norris can outfit you with overalls and a decent hat. You better get over to the blacksmith shop and see about them stamp-irons, right away."

"Got your mind made up that I'm goin' to work, ain't you?" the tramp said lazily.

"Nothin' else. You're needed, feller—and the work won't be strange to you. I'm plumb sure of that."

Jug-Handle smiled cryptically. "Mebbe not—All right, I'll see you later." With a careless wave of the hand, he sauntered away in the direction of the blacksmith shop.

Melody entered the Here's A Go and bought a cigar. Pee-Wee motioned him down the bar, out of earshot of the other customers in the saloon. "Find Jug-Handle?" he asked, after some preliminary conversation.

Melody nodded. "He's throwin' in with me—with the Rafter-S, that is. I aim to put him to work."

"Think it can be done?" Pee-Wee queried.

"I'm certain of it. While we were talkin', them three Du Sangs come up on us. I don't know how much they heard. Guy Du Sang made some war talk. Hugo's on the prod, too, for that matter, but he bopped down on Luke Du Sang when that hombre started to tell me his thoughts. I kind of feel Hugo don't want anythin' to break, yet."

"'Tain't that," Pee-Wee shook his head. "Things can't break too soon to suit Hugo, but he don't want the break to come in town, I'm guessin'. Vaca Wells has sort of turned against him. He's too smart to try and fight the whole town. He'll try to get you alone—him or his men. That's why I wanted to see you a minute."

"You know somethin', Pee-Wee?"

Pee-Wee shook his head. "Nothin' exact, Melody, but the three Du Sangs was standin' out front here, a few minutes before you entered. They had their heads together, and was makin' war-medicine, if I read the signs correct. What's up, I don't know, but look out for a trap of some sort."

Melody nodded dreamily. "I knowed a feller once what set a trap for a lobo wolf. Caught the lobo, too."

"What happened?" Pee-Wee asked. "Did he kill the wolf?"

Melody shook his head. "When this hombre closed in on the lobo, the critter proved too tough for him to handle. He had him in the trap, all right, but didn't dare come nigh enough to finish him. Th' lobo sunk his fangs in a coupla times. The feller was laid up for a spell."

Pee-Wee nodded. "If this hombre you mention had had more experience, he'd have shot the animile from a distance."

"He'd had the experience, all right, but he figured the lobo was catched so tight in the trap that it wouldn't put up no fight. Over-confidence, that was the feller's trouble. Over-confidence has spelt defeat for more'n one man— or men."

Pee-Wee looked curiously at the cowboy. "Any moral to this story you're relatin'?"

Melody nodded. "Don't count your wolves, even when they're catched. . . . The lobo in question escaped eventual."

Pee-Wee considered for a moment. "See that you do," he grunted. "And look out for shots from a distance."

"That thought," Melody smiled, "ain't original with you, Slim."

"I don't maintain it is," Pee-Wee said earnestly. "I'm just joggin' your mind. You're too damn careless. It won't do to get careless, more'n once—not with them Du Sang snakes."

"Reckon you're right." Melody was momentarily serious. "Take my advice, Pee-Wee, and keep the same thought in mind. You ain't none too popular with the Diamond-8——"

"Shucks!" Pee-Wee chuckled. "I don't matter. One way or another I can't help Norris much——"

"You've helped plenty, already, and I'm countin' on you for more help. Keep your ears peeled. Mebbe you'll hear somethin' I can use. . . . Well, I'm headin' out of town for a spell."

"Bound where?"

"Kind of figure to ride to the Slash-O and see if I can borrow a couple of hands, or so."

"Tell Buck Kirby you're gettin' my vote in this business. It might help."

"I'll do that. Thanks. And *adios*. I'll be seein' you."

"Take care of yourself, cowboy. *Adios*."

Melody nodded and departed for the hitch-rack. Before mounting Jezebel he glanced both ways along the street, in search of the Du Sang trio. Nothing was to be seen of the three, nor was there anyone in sight who looked as though he might be a sheriff.

"Them Diamond-8 coyotes is pro'bly in the Silver Spur, cookin' up some heap bad medicine for one red-headed hombre known as Melody Madigan," the cowboy mused. "Oh, well——"

He placed one foot in the stirrup and swung up to Jezebel's back. "Get goin', hawss. We're ramblin' some more."

Wheeling the mare, he started her off at a long, distance-devouring lope along the main thoroughfare. Passing the Silver Spur, Melody caught no sight of the Du Sang outfit. He kept going, reached the edge of town and guided the pony out across the range, on the hoof-beaten trail that stretched in the direction of Buck Kirby's Slash-O outfit.

By two in the afternoon, Melody was well on his way to the Slash-O, with about five miles yet to cover. East of Vaca Wells, the scenery was a trifle more rugged, thickly carpeted at spots with heaped fragments of splintered granite. At others, the yucca grew in profusion, giving way only now and then, to stretches of mesquite and chaparral.

This was all "up and down" country. The trail wound in and out among low hills. Occasionally, Melody saw small bunches of Slash-O stock, inter-sprinkled with a mingling of Lazy-V cows.

He had just reined Jezebel around a sharp bend in the trail, winding between two hills, when he glimpsed two riders cutting down through the mesquite on the rise of ground to his right. They were approaching rapidly, spreading out a trifle as they came on. It looked as though they were planning to cut off Melody's advance.

Melody drew reins to a cautious walk, and closely scrutinized the pair of riders. It took him but an instant to recognize them as Luke and Guy Du Sang.

"Damn 'em!" the cowboy chuckled ruefully. "They heard me tell Jug-Handle I was comin' out here. I reckon they figure to spoil all my fun, if they can." He considered rapidly: "Wonder if I better turn tail and run from 'em. It wouldn't be dignified, but it might be a heap more healthy."

He checked Jezebel, intending to wheel the mare and beat a hasty retreat. Then, he stopped. The two Du Sangs had caught the movement, and also brought their ponies to an abrupt halt. Simultaneously, the hands of each reached to the rifles in their saddle scabbards.

"Damn' if they ain't got me in a fix," Melody mused. "If I stick, they will drill me. If I run for it, they'll reach me with their smoke-poles. 'Course it ain't certain they'd kill me, but I wouldn't want to take no chances on it. No two ways about it, I'm cornered! Well, I might as well go down fightin' as runnin'. Wish I had a rifle, here. I'll stick. Mebbe I'll be able to talk 'em out of it."

He reined the mare around to face the two riders, and sat easily in the saddle waiting their arrival. The outlook was none too bright.

# 13. Roaring Guns

SEEING that Melody was making no move to escape, the two Du Sangs replaced their half drawn rifles in boots, and came thundering on. In a moment more they had come up with him, one on either side, where they jerked their mounts to haunches in a wild scattering of dust and gravel.

For a moment nobody spoke. On Melody's right was Luke Du Sang. The other brother had drawn to a halt on the left side of the cowboy. The faces of the two were plainly triumphant, despite their scowling features.

Suddenly, to their amazement, Melody grinned widely. "It was close," he announced, "but you win." He motioned to Guy Du Sang, on his left. "You win by a bridle-bit."

"What in hell you talkin' about?" Guy demanded.

"Your race," said Melody.

"What race?" from Luke.

"Wa'n't you two runnin' a race?" Melody queried blandly. "I see you both ridin' the hoofs off'n your broncs, so I figured right to once you was runnin' a race to see who had the fastest——"

"You know damn' well we wa'n't racin'," Guy Du Sang snarled. "We come out here a purpose to see you, Madigan."

"Thought you seen me in Vaca Wells."

Luke's voice was heavy with anger when he answered. "Not the way we wanted to see you, hombre. There's somethin'——"

"I see." Melody's tones were careless. "You didn't hear all of the conversation I had with Jug-Handle, and you want me to complete it for you. What's the matter, wa'n't one of you enough to come after the information?"

"One's enough, hombre," Guy Du Sang commenced, "but——"

"You keep your trap shut," Melody said suddenly, "or

I'll sprinkle you with insect powder! I'm talkin' to your brother. How about it, Luke?"

"You'll——" Guy choked and his voice ended in a sudden fit of cursing. His hand dropped to gun-butt.

"What a minute, Guy!" Luke's voice was stern. "Hugo put me in charge of this job." He turned to Melody, as Guy became speechless with rage. "Now look here, Madigan," Luke continued, "we don't want no trouble so we're givin' you a chance to vamoose. You're outta Vaca Wells now, and if you just keep goin', nobody's goin' to miss you much. It's up to you."

"An' supposin' I choose to stay?" Melody's voice was mildly curious.

Luke grinned wickedly. "That's what me and Guy come out to prevent," he rasped. "One way or the other—we ain't particular which—you ain't returnin' to Vaca Wells. What do you want to do?"

Melody looked thoughtful. "That sorta requires some thought," he stated slowly. He reached for Durham and papers, and at the movement the hands of the other two reached to hips. "Gotta smoke on it," Melody observed nonchalantly.

Guy and Luke relaxed their holds on gun-butts and eased a trifle. Melody sifted some tobacco into a paper and methodically twisted it into a smoke which he placed between his lips. His fingers groped in vest pockets for a match.

"You make it sorta hard for a feller," he continued in his slow drawl. "Me, I ain't hankerin' to die right away, yet I don't like to disappoint Norris."

The two Du Sangs backed their horses a trifle. Melody touched Jezebel with one spur, and the mare moved to take up the distance between her rider and the other two horses. Melody's mount was facing Guy Du Sang's pony now, shoulder to shoulder. The relative distance between Madigan and Luke remained the same.

"You know, after all, as I told you," Luke urged, "we don't want no trouble. You're suspectin' the Diamond-8 of a heap of things that ain't so, but rather than allow any mean suspicions to get around, we figure to see you out of the way, Madigan."

Madigan didn't appear to hear him. He was still searching for a match. Finally, he located one. "I don't like to disappoint Norris," he repeated slowly, scratching the

88

match. He touched the flame to the cigarette, inhaled deeply, then added in the same casual voice, "And I ain't intendin' to, neither, you buzzards."

His manner had thrown the two somewhat off guard. For a brief instant, neither moved a muscle. Melody drew the cigarette smoke deeply into his lungs and waited, breathless. Then, Luke's voice, flat, emotionless: "We might as well let him have it, Guy."

Events took place in swift succession, after that. Even as the words left Luke's lips, Melody dug in his spurs. Startled, indignant at the sudden assault, Jezebel plunged into Guy's horse, nearly throwing it off balance—enough at least to spoil Guy's shot!

At the same instant, Melody's hand streaked to leather. His gun flashed out as the little mare carried him past Luke. Luke's muzzle hadn't yet cleared holster, when a lance-like stab of white fire spurted from Melody's forty-five! Luke swayed drunkenly and pitched to the ground.

Melody felt the heat of Guy's bullet scorch his face! He whirled in the saddle. Guy Du Sang was raising his gun for a second try. Melody's Colt belched lead and flame, the abrupt burst of smoke mushrooming from the barrel!

A cry of anguish left Guy's mouth, as his right arm went limp. He caught the weapon in his left hand as it fell, started to raise it, then stopped.

Melody had the mare turned by this time, his forty-five covering Guy. Twin spirals of gray tobacco smoke curled from the cowboy's nostrils. It wasn't necessary for him to give an order. Guy slumped in the saddle and dropped his gun to the ground. Luke was sprawled face-down on the earth, his body twitching a trifle. That was all.

Melody laughed coldly. The tones seemed strangely soundless after the deafening roar of the heavy guns. "I oughta finish you two, now," Melody said, "but I ain't built to kill men in cold blood. Get down off'n that horse, Du Sang, and see if your brother is worth takin' to a doctor."

Guy climbed down, holding his broken arm, went to Luke and managed to turn him over. "He's still alive," Guy grated sullenly, "but I don't——"

Melody dropped from Jezebel's back, and after warning Guy to keep his distance, lifted the wounded man to the horse which stood nearby. There was a coiled rope at the saddle, and Melody, always keeping one eye on Guy, quickly lashed the unconscious man across the pony's back. Then he backed away and mounted Jezebel.

"Ain't you goin' to bind up this arm for me, Madigan?" Guy asked.

"Not a-tall," Melody replied definitely. "A broken wing won't prevent you ridin', and you can lead your brother's hawss behind and guide with your knees. You're both gettin' more of a chance than you deserve, so get goin' before I change my mind."

With considerable groaning, Guy Du Sang climbed back in the saddle, grasped the reins of his brother's mount, and wheeled the two horses toward Vaca Wells. For a moment he turned to face Melody, his face graying with pain. "You ain't heard the last of this, Melody," he grated. "If it's trouble you want, I'll see that you get it. Wait until Hugo hears——"

"Take them threats home with you," Melody cut short the tirade. "It wa'n't so many hours ago, Du Sang, that you was warnin' me what'd happen when *you* started in. Well, you've tried to start. How do you like the goin' so far? I'll do some warnin' myself. The farther you go, the rougher the goin' gets. Just paste that in your Stet hat!"

Guy glared his hatred for a moment, then spoke savagely to his horse, kicked it in the ribs and moved off without further words, leading behind him the pony with its unconscious burden.

Melody whistled softly as he sat witnessing the departure. "Whew! I sure enough had a four-leaf clover hangin' 'round me that time. I kinda figured them two would finish me, when I reached for my lead-slinger. Plumb lucky—that's me. Well, this ain't gettin' to the Slash-O."

He cast a last look at the Du Sangs, just disappearing around the bend in the trail, touched spurs to his pony and moved on.

# 14. Melody Gets Help

THE SUN was commencing to cast shadows ahead of him by the time he rode into the Slash-O ranch yard. Buck Kirby, owner of the outfit, was sitting on his front porch in his sock feet, when Melody rode in.

Kirby was a spare, grizzled man well past seventy, but his frosty eyes still sparkled with a youthful fire. "Howdy, stranger," he greeted. "Light an' rest your stern a mite. I'm Kirby."

Melody dropped the reins over Jezebel's head and slid down. "I'm Madigan."

Kirby rose to his feet, eyed the cowboy shrewdly a moment, then spat a long brown unerring stream at a horned toad that had strayed too near the porch. "Madigan, eh?" he said, as the toad scuttled out of sight. "Huh. Thought mebbe that's who ye was. I says to myself, I says, when I see ye ridin' in, 'Buck Kirby,' I says, 'I'll bet a mess of rattler's pups that that hombre comin' is the red-headed devil that's buckin' Hugo Du Sang.'"

"You thrun your loop correct as hell," Melody grinned. "But how did you know about me?"

"One of my boys was in town this mornin'. He come back with the news. But what's the fight about?" He shoved a chair in Melody's direction, as the cowboy ascended to the porch. "Let's hear the story."

"That's what I come to tell you," Melody replied, seating himself. "Mr. Kirby, this range is plumb scarce where real men is concerned, ain't it?"

Kirby's face hardened. "Meanin'?" he grunted.

"Meanin'," Melody said steadily, "that you're all sittin' by an' lettin' them Du Sang coyotes tromp on Tom Norris an' his daughter, and not makin' a move to prevent. Is everybody just plain yellow, or don't they give a damn?"

"H'mmm." Kirby spat another long, brown stream together with an expletive. "Hell's bells! I ain't heerd nothin'

91

'bout that. If Norris is havin' trouble, why don't he yell for help? 'Course, I did hear tell that him and Du Sang was experiencin' some hard feelin's over water, but I didn't reckon it amounted to nothin'.'"

Melody softened a little. "Mebbe it is news to you, at that," he said. "In the first place, Norris ain't the kind to yell, and in the second, Du Sang has had everybody so skeery of him that they ain't got the nerve to speak out loud. Mr. Kirby, has it ever occurred to you how plumb simple it would be to make Diamond-8 cows outa Slash-O stock?"

Kirby looked thoughtful, then his brows gathered in a frown.

"You under-half crop both ears. Du Sang gotches 'em," Melody pursued.

Kirby nodded slowly. "Never liked Du Sang much, but I don't think he'd do that," he said at last. "Fact is, we ain't lost no cows, to speak of, the last two years."

Melody hammered home his arguments. "For the simple reason that Du Sang wants to get Norris out of the way first. After that he'll start in on you and the Lazy-V, and what he'll do will be plenty."

"You got any proof of this, young man?" Kirby asked severely.

"Not as to rustlin', but they's plenty proof that Du Sang wants me to quit meddlin' with his ideas. His two brothers tried to stop me on the way here, but I didn't see it that way."

"Ye mean that ye crossed guns with Luke and Guy, and beat 'em to the draw? Both of 'em at once? Pshaw! I can't believe it."

"Guy's got a broke arm," Melody smiled. "I don't know how bad I plugged Luke. He was still unconscious when I pulled out."

Kirby was jumping up and down on his chair with excitement. "I wanta know, I wanta know!" he exclaimed.

Melody gave him the story. What is more, he related everything that had happened since his first meeting with Jerry Norris—of how Du Sang was trying to steal the Norris ranch, and all the rest.

The old man's eyes were blazing with honest indignation when Melody had concluded. For a few minutes he couldn't find words to express himself. Finally, "Yep, it takes a red-headed young devil like you to wake us folks up to a sense of our duties. We ought to be kicked, the hull pack and passel of us! The idee! Lettin' Du Sang get away with any sech onery snake tricks. Why, why, iff'n he got away with sech notions, he'd be runnin' us all off'n the range. Son, what you wantin' me to do? I got money——"

"It ain't money we're needin' so bad right now, as men," Melody cut in. "If you could spare a coupla good punchers, though, Mr. Kirby, we'd appreciate it a heap. You see——" He outlined briefly his ideas for the Rafter-S.

"Two men, eh?" Kirby nodded. "Ye can have 'em, and anythin' else ye want that I got. Lemme see, lemme see, who will I give you?"

"This is strictly a loan, you know," Melody reminded. "We ain't got no money for salaries, and we can't pay you back until the Rafter-S gets on a workin' basis——"

"Who said anythin' about salaries? Hell's bells! I'll pay the salaries, gladly. I'll be owin' ye that much, if ye clean out that nest of Du Sang snakes. I'll let ye have Clem Osborne and Matt Oliver. They're the best men I got, aside from my foreman, and have been with me a long time."

"Thanks. That'll be fine."

"The boys won't be in until supper time. You better stay and chow with us. Won't be long, now. Then I'll ride to the Lazy-V with you and talk to Vaughn. I've knowed Vaughn quite a spell, and I'll help ye put your idee across. He'll let ye have men, I'm purty shore."

"Gosh, that'll help a lot—and grub will taste right good, too."

At supper time, Melody met the Slash-O crew, which consisted of a foreman, six punchers and a cook. Kirby was a widower with no children, and always ate with his men in the cook shanty. He sketched briefly for the crew the various things that Melody had told him covering the activities of the Diamond-8.

"——while there ain't no proof of rustlin', against Du Sang, boys," he finished, "you can see real plain what'll happen if Du Sang succeeds in wiping out Tom Norris. I'm figurin' to loan Madigan two men to use on the Rafter-S. Them two is Matt Oliver and Clem Osborne."

Oliver and Osborne looked interested. They were a lean, sinewy pair bronzed by many seasons of cow country weather, both past thirty, and appeared to Melody to be very capable punchers.

"Suits me fine," Oliver said.

Osborne nodded, then added, "Why wouldn't a stamp-iron do a heap to prevent blottin'?"

"You get the idea right off," Melody smiled. "In fact, I've already ordered a couple for the Rafter-S. When you boys go through Vaca Wells, you could put in orders for Slash-O irons, if Mr. Kirby wants 'em."

"Danged right I do," Kirby agreed. "And I'm goin' to tell Vaughn to do the same. We been awful lax, and it's high time we tightened up this range a heap. Melody, you got any orders to give Osborne and Oliver? They're your hands, now."

"If it ain't askin' too much," Melody responded, turning to the two punchers, "I'd like to have you boys head for the Rafter-S right after supper. I'll feel a lot safer if I know Norris has got help, if needful."

Both agreed with Melody. "We'll get goin' in a short spell," Oliver added. "You mentioned a feller that you'd hired, called Jug-Handle, a while back. You don't mean that hobo that's been hangin' around the Here's A Go, do you?"

"The same," Melody smiled. "And don't underestimate him none. That hombre's got a right head on him. I've told him what I want done, so if I ain't back early tomorrow mornin', you talk to him. I'm aimin' to slope over to the Lazy-V tonight, and see if we can't get a coupla more waddies."

The talk drifted from subject to subject, always coming back to Du Sang, however. "Mebbe," one of the men ventured, "Du Sang knew somethin' about the killin' of that cattle dick that was down here a spell back."

"Now that you speak of it, Hen," Matt Oliver put in, "I allus did suspect somethin' queer about that. 'Course, when the body was found, a lot of hombres thought that dick had shot hisself by accident."

"It was Tom Norris, originally, asked the Association to send a man down here," Melody said. "Norris told me about it when I was out there. The first man that come down didn't have no chance to uncover anythin' before the Association had called him to another job. Then, the second man arrived. He wasn't here long before he was found dead on Diamond-8 range, I understand. The body was shipped back, but the Association hasn't sent another man yet. I'm sayin' this, because a heap of folks are thinkin'

94

that I'm a cattle dick. I'm tellin' you, flat out, that I ain't. I wish I was, though. The authority might come handy some day."

Supper was finished, cigarettes were lighted. The group at the long table broke up. Matt Oliver and Clem Osborne, with some final instructions from Melody, caught up their ponies and headed for the Rafter-S. A short time later, Melody and Buck Kirby headed south toward the Lazy-V.

It was considerable of a ride to the Vaughn outfit, and the hour was late by the time the two men arrived. They found George Vaughn still up, however.

Vaughn had all of the typical Englishman's natural reserve, but he greeted Melody cordially enough when Kirby introduced the two. The owner of the Lazy-V was a bachelor, nearly fifty, with smoothly-shaven features, crisp brown hair, and frank blue eyes. He was long-limbed and slim, with a terse, jerky manner of speech, and the usual broad *a's* of his race.

Courteously, he refrained from asking Melody's business until easy chairs had been arranged in the living room of the ranch house, and a squat brown bottle and glasses placed upon a table of comfortable proximity. A box of mellow Havanas was also produced and laid open for his guests.

"Don't mind Scotch, I hope," he jerked at Melody, filling the glasses. "Can't drink your beastly Bourbon. No seltzer, either. Sorry. Beastly country. No comforts. I like it. Can't get away from it, y'know." He lifted his glass, "Here we go."

The liquor was consumed, then Buck Kirby exploded, "George, you'n me are a pair of lousy pole-cats! In fact, dang near this whole range comes under that headin'."

Vaughn blinked rapidly. "Pole-cats? Pole-cats. Oh, I say, now!"

"Skunks, plain skunks!" Kirby made himself clear.

Vaughn's eyes hardened a trifle. "Oh, I say, old man, that's drawing it a bit fine, y'know," he protested mildly.

"Wait'll I tell you——" Kirby plunged into a long recital of the things he had learned from Melody. Vaughn heard him through in silence, breaking in only once to do things with the Scotch and glasses.

The story was finally concluded. Vaughn studied Kirby a moment, then turned shrewd, scrutinizing eyes on Melody. Finally, he nodded, "Oh, I say, that's a bit thick.

Not cricket, y'know." He reached to the table and procured his belt and gun which lay there, then, "This Du Sang person needs a bit of taking down, I judge. Where can one find the ruddy bounder at this moment?"

Melody grinned. He was liking Vaughn more all the time. "No use of you getting into this, personally, Mr. Vaughn, unless necessary," he suggested. "I'm askin' the loan of a couple of good hands, though. Mr. Kirby has been good enough to send two men to the Rafter-S. If you can do the same, I'll be appreciatin' it a heap, and so will Tom Norris. The best thing you can do is use stamp-irons when you're brandin', as Mr. Kirby suggested, and keep an eye on your own stock. If everybody left their own range to run to Norris' aid, Du Sang might be tempted to change his base of operations."

Vaughn nodded. "Quite. Quite. Quite right," he commented. "Naturally, you may have two men. Lee and Farrell. Young fools. Both of 'em. Like to fight, no end. Just the chappies for you. Miss their tiffin for a fight, any time, y'know. That sort. One minute."

He left the room and in a short time returned from the bunkhouse with two young cowboys whom he introduced as Mesquite Farrell and Tennessee Lee. They were about the same age as Melody; clean-cut, sinewy-jawed punchers with fun-loving reckless eyes.

Vaughn explained briefly. "Bit of a mess, y'know. Rafter-S. Norris. You two boys—help out. All that sort of thing. Clean the bounders off the range. Buck and Mr. Madigan will stay the night. Plenty of time for talk. Get another bottle when that's finished. Sit down."

Melody liked Vaughn's direct methods. The five men seated themselves about the table and talked far into the night. The next morning, after thanking Vaughn and Kirby, Melody started for the Rafter-S, accompanied by Tennessee Lee and Mesquite Farrell.

When halfway there, he sent the two punchers on alone, and wheeled his pony toward Vaca Wells. He wanted to learn how the news of his fight with the Du Sangs had been received—and any other news that Pee-Wee might have to offer.

**PART IV**

# *"Start Shootin' !"*

## 15.

IT WAS after eleven o'clock that same morning when Manitoba came striding into the Here's A Go. The place was empty, except for Pee-Wee, standing alone behind the bar.

Pee-Wee shuffled up to position. "What you drinkin', Manitoba?"

"Gimme a shot."

Pee-Wee served the drink, tossed the payment into his till, and eyed his customer with shrewd eyes. The Diamond-8 man was covered with dust, shirt soaked with perspiration, his face streaked with alkali where rivulets of sweat had coursed down from his forehead.

"You look like you'd been ridin', Manitoba," Pee-Wee ventured.

"Nobody asked you for your opinion," Manitoba growled. "As a matter of fact, I ain't been outta town since yesterday, if you gotta know."

"I ain't. Don't make no difference." Pee-Wee dismissed the subject with a wave of one pudgy hand, but nevertheless, held in reservation the idea that Manitoba was seven different kinds of a liar. "How's Luke?" Pee-Wee inquired after a moment.

"He'll live, I reckon," Manitoba grunted. "Guy's arm is broke, but I guess it'll heal clean. Hugo has took Luke out to the Diamond-8. That was certain a yellow dog's trick that Madigan pulled yesterday."

"Yeah? Ain't heard about it," said Pee-Wee.

"You know what I'm talkin' about, Pee-Wee. Madigan sneakin' up on Guy and Luke, like he done, and pluggin' 'em. Killed 'em outright if Guy hadn't druv him off."

Pee-Wee was plainly skeptical. "Who says so?"

"Luke and Guy. Both of 'em."

"Oh, that's it." There wasn't any variation in the degree of skepticism in Pee-Wee's voice. "Madigan got close enough to plug 'em with his forty-five, did he? Well, well. . . . Somethin' funny. I was talkin' to Doc Kenyon this mornin', and he told me they'd both been shot from the front. They must'a' been sleepin' when Madigan snuk up on 'em. Broad daylight too."

"Think you're almighty wise, don't you?" Manitoba sneered.

"I'm wise enough not to believe any such tale as that. I ain't seen Madigan since it happened, but I'm bettin' a stack of blues that he outfought, outdrew, outshot and outguessed, the two of 'em, and they're ashamed to admit it. What do you think of that, feller?"

"Aw, shut up an' gimme another drink."

Pee-Wee set out the bottle, but refused to shut up. "Furthermore, I been doin' a heap of thinkin'," he continued, "about what Guy and Luke was doin' over east of Vaca Wells when it happened. Yesterday, before he left, Melody come in here and told me he was goin' over and get acquainted with Buck Kirby. Next thing I hear is that Luke and Guy met him on the road and got plugged for their pains. Looks damn funny to me—as though they figured to ambush him and he got wise to their plans. Serves 'em damn well right, if that's the case. It's a wonder to me that Hugo ain't had somebody out looking for Melody to sorta try and avenge them wounds he handed the Du Sang brothers."

Manitoba started, glanced quickly at Pee-Wee. The proprietor of the Here's A Go didn't miss the movement, nor the guilty frown that passed across Manitoba's face, but his plump features remained as placid as ever. A breath of relief was softly exhaled from the Diamond-8 man's lips. Pee-Wee motioned to the bottle. "Have one on the house, Manitoba."

Pee-Wee was thinking fast, now. Manitoba rarely came into the Here's A Go, unless prompted by some ulterior motive. Pee-Wee had kept a continual watch on the doorway ever since Manitoba had come in. Things came clearer to the fat proprietor after a few minutes. Manitoba's dusty clothing clinched the idea that was taking form in Pee-Wee's mind: Manitoba had been out on the range, watching to learn when Madigan started toward Vaca Wells.

Manitoba knew that Melody would come first to the Here's A Go. And now the Diamond-8 man was waiting for Melody to enter the door, ready to shoot him down without warning. Hugo Du Sang's orders, undoubtedly; Hugo Du Sang's idea of evening the score for the shooting of his two brothers.

Cold perspiration burst suddenly on Pee-Wee's round face. A shudder ran through his body. He glanced at Manitoba who was helping himself to a drink. Gawd! What could he do to prevent the murder? Pee-Wee was realizing rather abruptly that he thought a lot of the fightin' redhead. And here stood this killer, ready to kill Melody the instant the cowboy entered the saloon.

Manitoba looked up suddenly, glanced curiously at Pee-Wee's fear-stricken face. "What's the matter, Pee-Wee? You look like your bank had failed, or somethin'."

Pee-Wee's grin was ghastly. "It—it ain't nothin'," he stammered, "only I just happened to—to think——"

"Don't strain your brain. Thinkin' is bad for some folks."

"Thinkin' is damn' expensive, if I don't think fast," Pee-Wee exclaimed with a burst of inspiration. "It just occurred to me that a feller reminded me this mornin' that that last bar'l of liquor I got, was leakin' all over my porch, out front. I plumb forgot it until just now. I should'a' brought it in when it first arrived."

He hurried down to the end of the bar—if a man so fat can be spoken of as hurrying—and started for the door. " 'Scuse me," he panted, "while I go 'tend to that bar'l. I don't want to lose all my profits."

He disappeared through the doorway. Manitoba looked after him, scowling. "Damn' fat fool,'" he muttered. "He's due to lose more than his profits, one of these days, soon. Reckon I'll have me another drink while he's gone."

A wide grin stretched Manitoba's thin lips as he proceeded to help himself to a goodly portion of whisky, direct from the bottle. He set it down with a satisfied smack. "That's one drink I won't pay for, anyhow. . . . Yes, that fat slop is due to pass out right sudden pretty quick, now. But Madigan comes first."

He gave himself over to thoughts of the contemplated murder. Madigan had still been some distance away, when Manitoba, hidden behind a rise of ground, had seen him leave two other riders and head toward Vaca Wells. Madigan should arrive now, any minute.

Manitoba's lips curled back in an animal-like snarl as he though of how he would shoot the cowboy down without giving him a chance to draw. There'd be one witness— Pee-Wee—as very few people frequented the saloon at this hour of the day. If necessary he's shoot Pee-Wee, too.

Manitoba dwelt on the thought. Shoot Pee-Wee, too. Hugo would like that. And if there was any fuss raised about the killing, Hugo could fix it with the sheriff. He'd fixed things before. Sheriff Higley was another fool, but he made a good tool for the Diamond-8, at times. Oh, yes, Higley was a handy man to have around.

Five minutes passed. Manitoba helped himself to another drink. At that moment Pee-Wee re-entered the saloon, and saw Manitoba with the bottle to his lips. "Don't hurry, feller," Pee-Wee remarked sarcastically. "You can have that bottle, I don't want it—now."

Manitoba laughed shortly. "Hell! I didn't hurt your bottle. Your liquor still leakin' outta the barrel, Pee-Wee?"

Pee-Wee waddled behind his bar, shook his head. "It's all right, I reckon. Stopped leakin'. I guess the moisture must'a' swelled the wood. I didn't lose only a quart, or so."

At that moment Melody's voice was heard out at the hitch-rack: "C'mon, Jezebel, you female imp of Satan, you can have that drink you been cravin'. Go on, stick your nose away in—deep—drown yourself, you hammer-headed horsehide full of perversity. See if I care."

"That's Madigan, now," Pee-Wee said nervously.

He glanced at Manitoba and saw that he had guessed a-right. The man had fallen into a half-crouch, both guns leveled in his hands, eyes glued on the doorway. Manitoba was ready to fire the instant Melody entered!

"Hey," Pee-Wee protested, "what you doin', feller?"

Without moving his eyes from the door, Manitoba spoke from the corner of his mouth. "Keep your mouth shut, Pee-Wee. This is my affair. One yelp outta you, and I'll drill you, sure as hell!"

Pee-Wee fell into silence. He looked first at Manitoba, then at the guns. He commenced to wish, now, that he hadn't loaned Jug-Handle that old forty-five.

The minutes slipped past. No sign of Melody, yet. Manitoba was growing uneasy. Perhaps Melody was standing out in front. Manitoba's breath commenced to come in quick, short pants. The strain of waiting was beginning to tell. Dammit! Why didn't that red-headed devil show up?

Still in a crouching position, Manitoba started to move toward the doorway, sliding along on the balls of his feet. His guns were cocked, ready for instant action.

He had almost reached the door, when soft laughter from behind fell on his ears. Then, "Drop them guns, Manitoba! You're covered complete!" Next, a nervous gasp of relief from Pee-Wee!

With a half-smothered curse, Manitoba dropped his guns to the floor, and whirled around to see Melody's grinning face. The explanation was instantly clear to the Diamond-8 man. Madigan had entered by the rear door of the saloon. Manitoba cursed himself for a fool. How in hell had he come to forget that back door?

Melody's voice was scornful. "What was you doin', Manitoba, stalkin' Injuns? Or was you aimin' to play cat and catch a mouse? There you was all doubled up like you had cramps, or somethin', watchin' that door. You wa'n't watchin' for me, was you?"

Manitoba shook his head. For a moment he couldn't speak. "No, no—I wa'n't watchin'— for you, Madigan," he managed to stammer at last. "It—it was a—a—another feller. I just wanted to play a joke on him." A sickly smile spread over his face, now green with fear. "You—you understand how it was, don't you?"

"Do I?" The two words cracked like rifle reports.

Manitoba gulped. "I—I was afeared you wouldn't understand, but—but shucks——"

With a lightning-like movement, Melody thrust his own Colts into holsters. "Pick up your guns, Manitoba. If you've got the nerve, start shootin'. If you ain't drift! This is your last chance. Next time we meet, I'll be rollin' lead. Think fast! What you aimin' to do?"

Manitoba bent forward and slowly picked up his guns, but he couldn't summon the requisite nerve to level them and pull triggers. For the moment his courage was gone. The sudden surprise had taken all of the fight out of him for the time being. Thumbs hooked into belts, Melody stood carelessly awaiting the man's first move. But it wasn't hostile when it came.

Manitoba lacked even the nerve to speak, now. He

turned slowly toward the door, slammed his guns into holsters, and lurched off down the street.

Melody turned gravely toward the bar, hand thrust out. "Shake, Jee-Wee," he said gravely. "I'm much obliged for the warnin'. That snake would'a' plugged me sure, if you hadn't seen me first."

"And he's li'ble to plug me yet," Pee-Wee laughed shakily, "if he happens to notice I ain't got no bar'l of whisky on my porch. I wonder did he think I was soppin' the leak up with a sponge, all that time I was outside waitin' for you."

# 16.
## Melody Plays a Strong Hand

For a short time questions and answers flew back and forth between the two. "I knew danged well," Pee-Wee told Madigan "that you'd outshot them two Du Sangs. I'm plumb tickled that they was on the receivin' end of your lead, 'stead of vicy-versy. You was lucky, though, boy. Them two has reputations for bein' fast."

"Uh-huh, I was lucky," Melody agreed. "They had me cornered, like a treed puma. I'm hopin' my luck holds."

"It's got to," Pee-Wee said stoutly. "Dang it! I wish I hadn't growed to hippo size. I'd sure like to fork a horse and throw lead, again. But shucks, here I am, tied to a wet goods shop. By the way, you better light out before the sheriff sees you. The Du Sangs has swore out a warrant agin you, chargin' you with assault and battery, murder, with intent to kill, and everythin' else they could think of. Somehow, they forgot to put in arson and kidnappin'. Course, Doc Kenyon has gone on record with the statement that both Luke and Guy was plugged from in front, but Higley might make trouble——"

"Who's Higley?"

"Sheriff—Big-Foot Higley."

"Oh, yeah, I forgot his name. I ain't seen him yet."

"You ain't had time to see nobody hardly, but you sure been movin' fast in the three days you been here. Seems like a week, anyhow."

Melody grinned. "I've had to move fast. It seems like every time I throw laig across saddle, I'm goin' some place in a hurry. Tough on Jezebel, but that little mare's able to stand it. An' now you says this Higley is on my trail."

Pee-Wee nodded. "He might make some trouble, but mostly he's just a big bag of wind. Does anythin' Du Sang tells him to do."

"Uh-huh. Well, I guess I'll drift along and see how things is comin' at the Rafter-S. I may not get in again

103

for a few days. Except to be plenty busy. If anythin' unusual happens, or if you have any more leaky barrels of liquor, send me word and I'll come a-runnin'."

Pee-Wee accompanied him to the door. He laid one hand on Melody's shoulder. "Be careful, son," he advised seriously. "You're buckin' a strong combination. I'd hate to see you go down." And then, somewhat ashamed at his burst of affection, he added gruffly, "But it'd serve you right, if you got shot all to hell. Meddlin' in folks' business the way you been doin'!"

Melody understood. He reached over and for an instant laid his hand on Pee-Wee's. "Don't worry, Slim," he said fondly. "I get what you're drivin' at. S'long."

Pee-Wee followed him out on the porch, as though reluctant to see him leave. Melody was just starting down the steps when Pee-Wee called him back.

"It's the sheriff—Big-Foot Higley," Pee-Wee explained in a whisper. "You'll have to face him, son."

Melody looked down the street and saw a large, full-bellied man approaching with important stride. On his vest the approaching man wore a somewhat tarnished star of office.

"Manitoba pro'bly told him you were here——" Pee-Wee commenced.

"Quick—what's his name? Not 'Big-Foot'—I mean his real name."

Pee-Wee pondered. "Damn' if I know—oh, yes—Martin S. I don't know what the S stands for."

"All right."

By this time Higley had neared the porch. He opened his mouth to speak, when Melody forestalled him, "Just the man I'm lookin' for," Melody greeted with a smile. "You're the sheriff of Vaca Wells, ain't you?"

"I am. I want you——"

"Well, that's great," Melody cut in enthusiastically. "I wanted to meet you. My name's Madigan." He seized the sheriff's hand and commenced to pump it up and down with considerable vigor.

Higley's mouth opened and shut like that of a fish out of water, but words wouldn't come. His vocal chords appeared to be paralyzed. "But—but—but——" he finally managed to blurt.

Melody didn't appear to hear him. "Martin S. Higley,

ain't it? Sometimes called 'Big-Foot'?" He renewed the handshaking. "Well, this is luck! Meetin' you first off, this-away, is more than I expected. As the governor says to me, he says, 'Look up Martin Higley, and——' "

The sheriff's eyes widened. "Do you know the governor of this State?"

"Know him?" Melody stared at the questioner as though it were an affront to doubt the fact. "Know him? Well, I should say I do! The governor and my ol' dad went to school together. He always thught a lot of me, so when I was passin' through the capital I dropped in and we had a coupla drinks and a real talk. You know how the governor is, Higley. Always tellin' funny stories. Well, he had one that was the best thing I ever heard. It was about two Swedes that——"

"Look here," Higley cut in, striving to be stern, "there's some things that don't look good——"

"Them's the very words the governor said," Melody interrupted. A troubled expression appeared on his features, his manner turned apologetic. "Gosh, Higley, I hate to say it, but them was the governor's very words. He said to me, 'Mel, my boy, there's some things that don't look good down in Vaca Wells. I've always heard that Martin Higley was a good law-officer, but I've been gettin' reports——' "

Melody broke off and stressed the matter. "Mind you, Higley, he's been gettin' reports on Vaca Wells, and the law enforcin' activities down here. Can you imagine that? A big man like the governor, goin' into details about a little town like this? But, that's like him. He's a great man for seeing the law enforced."

"Uh-huh, uh-huh," Higley nodded dumbly with no visible show of enthusiasm. "Wha—what was it he said about me?"

Melody looked the sheriff full in the eyes. "He said, 'Mel, my boy, I've heard there's a wild bunch runnin' Vaca Wells. Now, I've always thought Martin Higley was a good, upright man, the sort I want down there to enforce the law, but I don't like the reports that keep comin' in. So when you get down that way, Mel, drop in on Vaca Wells, and talk to Higley. If you think it necessary, I'll conduct an investigation, and if conditions is bad, we'll send the soldiers down there to run that wild bunch out.

If Higley can't get law and order, I'll have to remove him from office, that's all. But I hate to do it. I think he's a good man, though he may have been led astray.'" Melody looked serious. "Them's the governor's very words, Higley."

Higley drew out a bandanna and mopped his face. He looked worried, and the hand holding the handkerchief was unsteady. "There—there must be some mistake about them reports," he gasped weakly. "I don't understand—must be some mistake. I'm runnin' this town as tight as I know how. I wouldn't want no trouble about my job. I—I—well, you see, Madigan—I——"

Melody frowned. "Well, I dunno, Higley. It might go hard with you, if you were indicted. I hate to say it, but things don't look as lawful around here as they might. Why, the first day I was here, a feller by the name of Badgely tried to murder me. Mebbe you heard about that. And then, there was some other——"

"That's all right—all right," Higley said nervously. "That was self-defense. I intended to speak to you about the shooting of the Du Sang boys, but the doctor tells me they was both shot from the front, so I don't know——" His voice trailed off rather vaguely.

"I just seen that Manitoba feller with a gun in his hand, a short time back," Melody pursued easily. "He said as how he was aimin' to play a joke on somebody, sheriff, but I dunno. It looked sorta funny to me, like he might have been intendin' to shoot somebody. You and your deputy oughta keep an eye on such fellers."

"Ain't got no deputy," Higley said. "I just deputize fellers as I need 'em. That's pro'bly what the governor meant. You see, I been tryin' to save money for the county, and it may be that I bit off more than I can chew. I'll just have to be a mite more strict with the boys, that's all. I wouldn't want to cause the governor no worry."

"That would be bad," Melody agreed gravely.

"I wish—I sorta wish when you write him," and there was a pleading note in Higley's voice, "that you'd tell the governor I'm doin' my best down here, and that it won't be necessary to conduct an investigation, nor nothin'."

"I'll be glad to do that for you, Higley," Melody replied soberly, "so long as you assure me that things will run smooth here. I wouldn't want to see you lose your job

106

and get into a lot of trouble. Well, I'm certain glad we had this talk. Have a drink, sheriff?"

Higley shook his head. "Much obliged, but I reckon not," he refused piously. "I ain't a drinkin' man. Thanks jest the same. If there's anythin' I can do for you, Mr. Madigan, just say the word. Good-bye."

He quickly turned away and walked rapidly down the street, considerably shaken by the turn events had taken.

Pee-Wee stared after the retreating figure in amazement. "Not a drinkin' man," he repeated. "Why, that ol' liar!" He laughed until his fat sides shook like jelly. "Melody, you sure played a strong hand that deal. He was aimin' to arrest you when he come here, too. I saw the warrant stickin' out of his pocket. But Big-Foot Higley knows better than to tangle with a friend of the governor's. Cowboy, you just plain scared him outta his taste for liquor. He'll be gettin' religion, next."

Melody grinned widely. "I had to do somethin' fast. I want to get out to the Rafter-S—not spend the night in jail."

"Well, you sure stopped him," Pee-Wee chuckled. "By the way, Melody, what's the governor's first name? I was tryin' to think of it the other day."

Melody had already started for the hitch-rack. He turned slightly, speaking over on eshoulder. "How do I know, Pee-Wee?" he drawled. "I ain't no votin' politician."

Light suddenly dawned upon Pee-Wee. "You mean to say you don't know the governor, a-tall?" he demanded. "Why, you young liar! You was just bluffin' Higley!"

"Guilty," Melody admitted, swinging into the saddle. He nodded, "See you some more, Big Boy," and swung into a swift canter that carried him rapidly down the street.

Pee-Wee looked after the diminishing figure. "Damn' if that kid ain't the limit," he chuckled. "I sure wish he was my own boy, 'cause I could be right proud of ownin' a younker like him."

He turned slowly and waddled back into the interior of the saloon.

# PART V

## *Manitoba's Revenge*

### 17.

FROM a position a short distance down the main street of Vaca Wells, Manitoba had witnessed Higley's arrival and somewhat crestfallen departure. A few minutes later the Diamond-8 man had seen Melody ride away, laughing.

"Damn that thick-headed sheriff," Manitoba muttered. "Wonder why he didn't go through with the business? He looked like Madigan had put the bee on him, somehow. . . . I hate to think what Hugo is goin' to say. Luck is shore breakin' against us."

He hustled down the street and entered the Silver Spur Saloon. Sheriff Higley was standing at the bar when Manitoba entered. The sheriff flushed crimson, then noting the angry look on Manitoba's scowling features, half turned away, as though not wanting to talk.

There were only two or three customers in the Silver Spur at the time and they were engrossed in conversation with the barkeeper. Manitoba rocked sullenly across the plank floor of the saloon, and dropped into a chair at a table in one corner.

"Higley," he jerked out, "come here. I want to talk to you."

Higley turned uneasily to face the Diamond-8 gunman. "Sure, Manitoba," he nodded, crossing the barroom. "What's on your mind?" Drawing out a chair, he sat down across the table, repeating, "What's on your mind?"

Manitoba gazed contemptuously at the sheriff a moment before saying, "Lost your nerve, eh?"

"Wh—what do you mean?" Higley stammered.

"Just what I said. Hugo swore to that warrant, yesterday, after Guy brought Luke in. You was to arrest Madigan the minute he showed up. You yellow louse——"

"Look here," Higley blustered, "you can't talk to me that way, Manitoba. I ain't takin' that from no man——"

"You'll take that and a lot worse," Manitoba interrupted ominously. "Why didn't you arrest——"

"Why didn't you go through with your plans?" Higley bridled. "You told me this mornin' that you'd take care of Madigan and that it wouldn't be necessary for me to serve my warrant. I was watchin' down the street, waitin' to hear shots. Instead, I see you comin' out of the Here's A Go, lookin' like a whipped dawg. An' I'd seen Madigan arrive a few minutes before——"

"Shut your mouth!" Manitoba half rose from his chair, right fist clenched angrily.

Higley turned pale before Manitoba's wrath and shrank back from the look in the killer's eyes. "All right, 'Toba," he voiced weakly. "No use you'n me goin' on the prod."

Manitoba dropped back in his chair, muttering sullen threats. "I didn't kill Madigan, because I changed my mind," he lied in ugly tones. "I got to thinkin' that mebbe it would be better to do things up, accordin' to law. I figured you was a big enough man to fill your office, but I see you wa'n't. What happened to take your nerve away?"

"It's the governor——"

"What governor?" Manitoba snapped.

"Governor of this state," Higley explained meekly. "He's a friend of Madigan's. The governor has been gettin' reports on Vaca Wells and conditions here. He's threatenin' to send soldiers down, if I don't take care of my duties right. He sent Madigan down here to check up on me."

Manitoba swore at him. "Do you believe that, you fool?"

"Certain, why not?"

"Hell, Madigan's run a whizzer on you. He's bluffed you eight ways from the ace. Bluffed you 'til you backed down. Made a fool out of you, Higley—if you could be any more fool than you are——"

"But the governor said——"

"Use your head, Higley. A politician like the governor ain't goin' to bother himself about what goes on here. He's too busy. Besides, no governor means anythin' in my life. Now, look here, Madigan's rid out of town. Gone to the Rafter-S, most like. You fork your hawss and ride out there and serve that warrant."

Higley shook his head. "Not me, 'Toba. I can't run no

110

chances on the soldiers bein' sent down here. How do you know so much about it? You didn't talk to Madigan. He repeated to me every word the governor had told him. I could see he knowed what he was talkin' about. No, siree, you don't get me meddlin' in no more such affairs."

Manitoba ripped out a violent oath. "I'd hate to be in your shoes, when Hugo hears about this."

"Can't help it," Higley said uneasily. "I don't reckon Hugo is strong enough to buck the cavalry if the governor sends 'em ridin' here to protect——"

"Look here, Higley, you give me that warant, and deputize me. I'll serve it." He smiled evilly. "I don't promise to bring my prisoner back here, though."

"Nope, I won't do that, neither, 'Toba. You best let things lay peaceful for a spell. I ain't takin' no more orders from Hugo Du Sang——" stubbornly, "——leastwise until maters has calmed a mite."

Manitoba jumped from his chair, cursing Higley for a yellow, spineless coward, but the words brought no response from the frightened sheriff, beyond, "Let's take a drink and forget it, 'Toba."

"I ain't drinkin' with no jelly-spined hombre like you," Manitoba snarled heatedly. He jerked around and strode out of the saloon.

Burning with baffled rage at Higley's refusal to help, and with anger at the manner in which Madigan had defeated his plans, Manitoba walked swiftly along the sidewalk, his thoughts in a red chaos of passion. An insane determination to make someone suffer obsessed his whole being. Manitoba was still wondering why Melody Madigan had chosen to enter the little-used back entrance of the Here's A Go Saloon at that particular moment; especially when the cowboy had been out in front, at the hitch-rack, a few minutes before. Manitoba cursed in a throaty growl, and stamped on along the sidewalk.

He commenced to suspect that he had been tricked in some manner. Melody must have been warned. But who could have warned the cowboy? Manitoba had spoken to no one of his murderous intentions. Hugo was the only one who knew of them. In fact, they had been formed at Hugo's insistence, in the event Higley's part failed. Manitoba's face burned redly. By this time he should have been on his way to the Diamond-8 with news of Madigan's

111

death. Hugo would sure raise hell this time, when he heard of the failure. Manitoba hated to face Hugo, now.

Something had to be done to square himself, that was all. Manitoba pondered, and pondering, commenced to perspire freely at thought of the things Hugo Du Sang would say. Manitoba, for all his badness, feared Du Sang's vitriolic tongue. And now, that yellow Higley was commencing to acquire a streak of law and order. Hugo wouldn't like that, neither.

It was at the moment Manitoba was passing the Here's A Go that an idea suddenly came to him. He happened to glance at the broad porch of the saloon. Something clicked in his brain. What was it? Oh, yes. That leaky barrel of whisky. Manitoba shook his head impatiently and started on. Then he stopped again. Strangely enough, there wasn't any whisky barrel on the saloon porch. In fact, there wasn't a box or barrel of any kind there!

The blood rushed to Manitoba's head. Everything was clear, now. It was that damn Pee-Wee Page who had guessed what Manitoba was about to do, and then, under the pretense of examining a leaky barrel, had gone to the street to await Madigan's arrival. It was Pee-Wee who had warned Madigan! Pee-Wee who had witnessed the whole humiliating affair and who would, doubtless, tell the tale all over Vaca Wells! Pee-Wee who advised Madigan to enter by the back door!

A lurid string of oaths poured from Manitoba's lips. His hand fell to gun-butt. He wheeled and started for the Here's A Go. Then, he checked himself. No, that wouldn't do. Vaca Wells would term it murder, and now, with Higley showing a yellow streak, Du Sang might not be able to fix any more murders. No, it would have to be accomplished in some other way.

Manitoba continued his course past the Here's A Go, then abruptly turned back and headed toward the Silver Spur Saloon, a revengeful plan formulating in his hate-warped brain. His horse was tied at the hitch-rack in front of the Silver Spur. Manitoba entered the saloon, and found Higley still seated at the table where he'd left him.

"I'm on my way back to the Diamond-8, Higley," Manitoba announced. "Have you changed your mind about arrestin' Madigan, or do you want me to tell Hugo you've lost your nerve?"

Higley squirmed. "I'd sure like to accommodate Hugo," he whined, "but honest to Gawd, Manitoba, I don't dare do it. Tell Hugo he better go easy for a spell, or——"

"Aw, you make me sick!" Manitoba growled disgustedly. "Right now, when you're needed the worst, you get a rush of chill to the feet." He laughed sarcastically. "All right, Big-Foot, it's your funeral, but you'll get hell when I tell Hugo what you said—and I'll tell him! Mebbe you won't be so stubborn after Hugo spills a mite of information about some of the things you've pulled in Vaca Wells. *That* will call for an investigation! You're plumb li'ble to find yourself in a stone apartment with barred windows——"

"Gawd! Manitoba, don't say that. I gotta keep things lawful here, for a spell. I simply gotta. Make it clear to Hugo the kind of a fix I'm in."

"I'll make it clear, all right," Manitoba threatened grimly. "I'll see that you get yours—plenty! Just wait until the gang learns how you've played traitor to 'em."

Higley put out one restraining hand, caught Manitoba by the sleeve, but the Diamond-8 man shook him off and strode toward the door.

Regardless of two other customers in the saloon who were eyeing him curiously, Higley followed Manitoba to the street, begging and pleading.

"Don't put me in wrong with Hugo, now, will you, Manitoba? I allus been a good friend of yours, ain't I? Just tell Hugo how it is. Ask him to gimme a coupla days to think it over, anyhow——"

Manitoba jerked roughly away, climbed into the saddle and wheeled his pony. "I'll tell him, don't worry," he jeered. "Wait until I get through tellin' him. I wouldn't be in your boots for nothin', Higley."

Sick at heart, perspiring with fear, the sheriff watched Manitoba, until the Diamond-8 man had disappeared from sight at the edge of town, and struck off across the range on the trail that led to the Du Sang ranch. Then, Higley directed his lagging steps back into the Silver Spur where he proceeded to get blindly drunk.

Once out of town, Manitoba swung off the trail. "Higley saw me ride out," he mused. "That'll be a strong alibi, regardless of anybody else who may see me return."

He circled wide and came back, re-entering Vaca Wells

113

by one of the cross streets, after drawing a bandanna well up across the lower part of his face. The bandanna, presumably, was to prevent dust and alkali from entering his throat and nostrils, but it also served as somewhat of a disguise. Enough, at least, to prevent a witness making sure of his identity.

Manitoba passed a few pedestrians on the street who paid him no attention, and entered the alley that ran back of the Here's A Go. A few minutes later he had jerked the bandanna down on his chest, dismounted at the rear of the saloon, and entered the building by the back entrance, closing the door behind him.

He grunted with satisfaction, upon noting the saloon to be empty of customers. Pee-Wee loked up, something of surprise in his face. "Back again, eh, Manitoba? What you drinkin'?"

If the proprietor of the Here's A Go noted the murderous gleam in Manitoba's eyes, there was nothing in Pee-Wee's manner to denote that fact.

"Gimme a shot of lightnin'," Manitoba replied. Pee-Wee turned to the back shelf. Manitoba continued across the floor to the front door which he closed and bolted. Then he swung back to the bar.

"Hey, what's the idea of lockin' my door?" Pee-Wee protested. "I get little enough trade as it is."

"I want to talk to you personal for a few minutes," Manitoba grunted. "I don't aim to be bothered." He tossed off his drink, then snapped, "Get your gun, Pee-Wee!"

"Can't do it—loaned it to Jug-Handle. I dunno——"

"That's your hard luck." Manitoba grinned wickedly. "Thought you was pretty smart, didn't you, Pee-Wee? Bah! You and your leaky barrel of whisky." His voice careened off into a high-pitched snarl. "Damn you! It was *you* warned Madigan I was waitin' for him!"

Pee-Wee paled and braced his hands against the bar. He had read his fate in Manitoba's eyes. But the fat man wasn't without nerve. He laughed scornfully. "Yeah, it was me, Manitoba," he admitted steadily. "Just loan me one of your guns, and I'll give you your chance to even the score. The boy was worth it—and he'll live to stop your dirty games. The Du Sang crowd is just about at the end

114

of its rope. But, gimme one of your guns. That's all I ask. You're faster'n me, but Melody will square——"

The sentence was never finished. Manitoba, a savage curse on his lips, had drawn and fired!

That one shot was enough to finish it, but for the moment, Manitoba went insane. Fiendish lights glittering in his eyes, he saw Pee-Wee wince as the bullet ripped through living flesh, saw the big man sag back against the shelf behind the bar. Then, deliberately, Manitoba raised his forty-five a second time: twice it belched flaming lead! Pee-Wee's eyes widened, he turned half around, then slumped to the floor, one grasping hand slipping along the bar in a futile effort to prevent the fall.

Smoke drifted in a low haze through the saloon. Manitoba quite suddenly realized what he had done. With an oath he jerked the bandanna back over his nose, thrust his still-smoking gun into holster, and leaped for the back door.

The next moment he was in the saddle, beating his horse furiously over the head with one clenched fist. In the street, paralleling the alley, he heard excited cries, but he saw no one. A moment more and he reached the thoroughfare by which he had entered the town. Plunging spurs into the pony's quivering hide, he headed for open range. So far, his plans had been executed without a slip. Escape seemed certain.

## 18.
## "I'm Gunnin' for Manitoba?"

THE NEWS reached Melody at the Rafter-S shortly after supper. His face went grim, then, with a few words of explanation, he saddled up his pony and started on a run for Vaca Wells. He was riding like one possessed, and it was no time at all before Jezebel had outdistanced the horse of the messenger who had brought the word of the tragic events of the day from the doctor in Vaca Wells.

Arriving in town, Melody went straight to Doctor Kenyon's house, where Pee-Wee had been carried. Darkness had fallen, and Kenyon led the cowboy to a bedroom lighted by a single oil lamp. Here, the fat man's bulk sagged motionless on an old-fashioned wooden bed.

"I don't know whether he'll regain consciousness again, or not," Doctor Kenyon was saying. "They brought him here and he opened his eyes just long enough to ask for you. I sent a man riding at once——"

"Who done it?" Melody demanded, his voice brittle with chill.

Kenyon shrugged his thin shoulders. "We don't know. There are a few who think it was suicide. The front door of the saloon had been locked. The men who were drawn by the sound of the shots, had to enter by the back way."

"Suicide nothin'," Melody snapped. "Pee-Wee's only gun is loaned to Jug-Handle. They wa'n't no gun found by the body, was they?"

"No—no gun found," Kenyon answered, shaking his head of iron-gray hair. "I think, myself, it is murder."

"No hope for him, eh?" Melody asked next.

"Not a chance. I don't understand why he's lived this long. Ninety-nine times out of a hundred, such wounds would kill instantly. I presume that's what the murderer figured on. No, Pee-Wee's finished. At best, I give him

116

two hours more. At times his pulse seems to stop completely, then it commences again."

"Did you get the slugs?"

"No use probing for them. It wouldn't help——"

Melody nodded his understanding. "In case I don't learn who done it, I wish you'd go after them slugs, Doc. I want to see what caliber they are. Might get a clue there. I'm goin' out, now. Be back shortly."

Melody departed and headed for the Silver Spur where the doctor had told him Sheriff Higley was. Higley had been too drunk to come to the Here's A Go when the tragedy occurred. Melody was suspecting Manitoba.

The cowboy found Higley sprawled over a table in the Silver Spur, sound asleep. He awakened him abruptly. The sheriff was a trifle more sober, now, but not much, as he eyed Melody with owlish gaze. "Oh, ish you, Misser Ma'igan. Fren' of governorsh. Thash me, too. Goo' fren' governorsh. You write letter to—governor—tell him Martin Higley goo' fren'——"

"Snap out of it, Higley!" Melody exclaimed. He enforced the order with a sharp slap across the sheriff's face, in an effort to shock him into sobriety. It didn't help much, although it did furnish some amusement for the patrons of the Silver Spur.

Higley shook one waggish finger reprovingly at Madigan. "Now, don' play rough, Misser Ma'igan. Governor wouldn't like it. You'n me—be goo' frensh, eh?"

Thoroughly disgusted, Melody straightened up, seized the sheriff by the collar and half-carried, half-dragged the limp-legged man through the doorway to the open air. But fresh air wasn't enough to overcome the tremendous amount of liquor Higley had consumed. Melody called for a bucket of water, while the sheriff clung for support to one of the uprights that held up the saloon porch wooden-awning.

There came a rush of feet at Melody's request. Three laughing men, quick to catch the idea, returned with as many buckets of water. Melody lifted the first bucket, emptied it over the drink-sodden sheriff. Higley gasped, slipped and fell down. A roar of laughter went up from the spectators who had gathered around.

Struggling, fighting for breath, Higley sprawled on the wet porch floor. Melody laughed grimly. Two more buckets of water followed the first. Then, Melody seized the rapidly-sobering man and jerked him to his feet.

"Wha—what's the idea," Higley sputtered. "Oh, it's you, Mister Madigan. But I don't——"

"Now, listen to me, Higley," Melody spoke sternly. "Pee-Wee Page has been murdered. Where's Manitoba?"

Higley blinked dumbly. "Pee-Wee murdered. Didn't know nothin' about it. Why didn't they tell me——"

"They did. You were too drunk to know it. Where's Manitoba?" The words were sharp.

"Manitoba? Oh, yes, Manitoba. Well, he ain't here. Went back to the Diamond-8, just a short spell after I talked to you, today."

"You sure of that?"

Higley nodded. "Saw him ride out of town."

Melody gazed steadily into the sheriff's bloodshot eyes, saw he was telling the truth. "All right, Higley. Now you better go get some sleep and complete that soberin' process I started. Hell's likely to break around here right soon. Don't drink no more."

"Hell goin' to break?" Higley repeated the words dully, his mind still clouded with alcohol.

But Melody didn't hear him. He was already on his way down the street. At the livery stable he procured a lantern, lighted it and headed for the Here's A Go. Somebody had had sense enough to lock the doors when Pee-Wee had been carried away, so Melody didn't try to enter. He made his way around to the back, and by the light of the lantern, studied the "sign" he found there.

There wasn't much to go on. Melody saw boot-prints where a man had entered and departed, the departing prints being spaced widely apart, showing that the murderer had been running. There was also evidence to show that a horse had been waiting there. That was all Melody could glean from the trampled earth.

Voicing a silent prayer that Pee-Wee might regain consciousness, if only long enough to tell who had shot him, Melody returned the lantern, and again bent his steps toward the doctor's house.

The stricken man was still breathing when Melody arrived. Some spark of life in the huge body struggled stubbornly against extinction.

"He'll go before midnight, sure," Kenyon prophesied.

But midnight came and passed, and still Pee-Wee lingered on.

"I don't understand it," the doctor exclaimed. "I've never seen such tremendous vitality."

"He's a big man in more ways than one," Melody replied gravely.

"That'll make a good epitaph."

The two fell silent. An old clock on a nearby shelf ticked off the minutes and lengthened them to hours. Death approaching on cat feet was making slow progress. Two o'clock came, then three, with no movement of any sort from the bed. Gradually, objects in the room became defined in thin gray lines. Melody glanced toward a window, caught a faint flush of rose-amethyst tinging the eastern sky.

"Mornin', doc," he announced tonelessly. "How much longer?"

Kenyon shook his head. "I lost faith in my knowledge some-time back."

The blanketed bulk on the bed stirred the covers. Both men were instantly on their feet. Pee-Wee's eyes were open. Something of a smile curved his lips as he looked at Melody.

"Pee-Wee, Pee-Wee, old friend," Melody cried. "Do you know me?"

"Certainly I know you, you red-headed devil," came the unexpected reply. "I ain't forgettin' that mug of yours——" His voice faltered, and for a moment his eyes closed, then opened again.

Kenyon held a spoonful of stimulant to the man's bloodless lips. "This is a pow'ful cold bed, Doc," Pee-Wee whispered a second later. "My laigs is like ice——" He broke off, chuckled weakly. " 'Taint your bed that's to blame, a-tall. I know—now."

"Pee-Wee, who done it?" Melody queried eagerly.

The dying man was fighting hard to retain his grip on life. He stared glassily at Melody. "You—you get the Here's A Go, son. It's yours. I ain't got—no relatives to leave it to—I want you to have—anythin' I got——"

"Pee-Wee, tell me! Who done it?" Melody was exerting every ounce of his will to hold the dying man to consciousness. "Who done it, who done it?" he was repeating over and over.

Suddenly, Pee-Wee sat upright. "Manitoba—but nev' mind that. Clean out—the Du Sangs first—Give 'em hell, son. You—can do——"

Quite abruptly his eyes closed and he fell back. Melody sprang forward. "I'll do it, Pee-Wee," he promised fervently, seizing Pee-Wee's hand. For a moment he felt a fierce tightening of icy fingers on his own, then it was all over.

Melody straightened up, eyes moist. "And that's that," he muttered unsteadily. "Doc, will you make arrangements with the undertaker? I gotta be goin'."

Kenyon looked curiously at the cowboy, who was just jamming on his sombrero. "Where you goin'?"

"Good God! Where am I goin'?" Melody's laugh was ugly. The fire in his gaze had dried the cowboy's eyes. "I'm gunnin' for Manitoba—where else would I be goin'?"

Kenyon leaped forward, seized Melody by the sleeve. "Now, be reasonable, cowpunch. Manitoba's at the Diamond-8, surrounded by his friends. I was out there, yesterday, attending to Luke Du Sang. I tell you, Madigan, you're mighty unpopular with that crowd. It's as much as your life is worth for you to go there at a time like this. There's the law to handle such cases. We'll make Higley arrest Manitoba and bring him to trial——"

"Trial?" Melody's voice was scornful, harsh. "You tryin' to preach law for a snake like Manitoba? Hell! Kenyon, Pee-Wee was my friend. Can't you realize that? Law courts don't satisfy in a case like this——"

"Don't be a fool, cowboy. You'll be outnumbered! You'll have to fight the whole Diamond-8 outfit, to say nothing of Manitoba. And Manitoba's bad!"

Something of a sob in Melody's laugh, now. "Bad? Manitoba bad? He ain't goin' to know what badness is, until he faces my guns!"

Impatient to be gone, he wrenched savagely away from the doctor's restraining grasp, and plunged out of the house. Kenyon turned his worried face back to the room where the dead man lay. "Pee-Wee, old scout," the doctor spoke to the lifeless clay, "if ever a man went berserk, it's Madigan at this minute, but I'm powerful afraid he's taken on too much of a job. Trying to avenge you will only result in his own death!"

The sun was up, now. A narrow shaft of yellow light

entered the window and fell softly across the dead man's face. It gave his features the appearance of having settled into a queer listening attitude. Perhaps Pee-Wee was hearing the staccato thudding of hoofs that carried Melody rapidly toward the Diamond-8. Or he may have been listening for the roaring of forty-fives. Who knows?

# 19. Guns of Vengeance

EIGHT men sat about a long table eating breakfast in the mess room of the Diamond-8 ranch. Hugo Du Sang sat at the head of the table; to his right was Guy Du Sang, one arm in a sling. Manitoba occupied a chair to Hugo's left. The other five were Fargo Phelps, Hub Wheeler, Tate Munson, Calico Worden and Squint Cantrell. Hard looking punchers, these five, fit employees for their crooked chief. Luke Du Sang was confined to his bed in the big, two-story ranch house, some hundred-odd yards distant from the mess shanty.

Hugo Du Sang spoke to the Chinese cook who shuffled about the table, refilling coffee cups. "Better fix up a tray for Luke, Chino, with the things Doc Kenyon ordered. And none of your damn' grease, mind. I'll take it up to the house when it's ready."

The Chinese cook smirked and bobbed, finished with the coffee-pot, and scuffed back to his kitchen to struggle with the intricacies of toast and beef broth.

"How's Luke feelin' this mornin'?" Tate Munson asked.

"Purty sore," Hugo answered. "He'll pull through, though. Already he's cravin' to cross guns with Madigan, again."

"Madigan's my meat," Guy Du Sang snapped. "Jest as soon as this arm heals——"

"Both of you better lay off'n Madigan," Hugo growled. "He'll be li'ble to finish you, next time."

"Aw, he ain't so much," Guy replied sullenly. "It was just that he took us by surprise, and my damn bronc wouldn't hold still. I shot before he did."

"The fact remains," Hugo pointed out, "that Madigan is still kickin' hell out of our game. I reckon I'll have to go after him myself."

"Gimme a shot at him, chief," Fargo Phelps said hopefully.

The answer was a scornful laugh. "Hell! Fargo," Hugo sneered. "He'd be through rollin' his lead, before you knowed they was a fight. You all admit that Manitoba's the fastest gun workin' for me, and yet you saw how Manitoba fell down on the job."

"Yeah, more surprises," snickered Calico Worden. "Manitoba, you must'a' looked plumb comical waitin' for him at the front door, and him standin' behind you all the time."

"That'll be enough from you, Calico," Manitoba said peevishly. "If it hadn't been for that damn' Pee-Wee, our troubles would be over. But Pee-Wee won't butt in on our game no more."

Hugo Du Sang looked a trifle concerned. "I'll feel a hell of a lot better when we get some news from town," he said slowly. "You're sure nobody didn't recognize you, eh, Manitoba? With Higley showin' a yellow streak, like you said, I won't be able to fix nothin', if they was any witnesses."

"Well, what the hell!" Manitoba blustered. "It was a fair fight. I've told you a dozen times. Everythin' was just like I said. I got a good alibi with Higley, too. Told him I was ridin'. He saw me leave town. Then I circled back and come in the back way of Here's A Go. I accused Pee-Wee of warnin' Madigan, and he saw they wa'n't no use to deny it. Instead, he reaches for his gun. I beat him to the draw, that was all. Then, I high-tailed it outta town."

"No chance of Pee-Wee livin' long enough to tell who done it, eh?" Hub Wheeler speculated.

Manitoba directed one contemptuous glance at the speaker. "When you've thrun as much lead as I have, Hub, you'll know how to finish your man pronto. Hell! I'm bettin' Pee-Wee was croaked before he hit the floor." He scowled uneasily. "What the devil is all the fussin' about, anyhow? What if they do find out I done it? Even if Hugo can't fix it, and Higley arrests me, what of it? They ain't got nothin' on me. Ain't I told you it was a fair fight? No jury's going to convict a man that shoots in self-defense. It was Pee-Wee or me."

Fargo Phelps looked dubious. "Mebbe it's just as you say, Manitoba, but I never knew Pee-Wee to pack a gun."

"He never wore it, but he always kept a gun on the shelf under his bar," Squint Cantrell put in.

"I dunno where his gun was," Manitoba lied sulkily, "but when I see him reachin' for it, I plugged him. Heard it fall on the floor. You hombres gimme a pain. It's me that rubbed him out, and if you ain't willing to back me up in case of trouble, you can go to hell! Nobody's got anythin' on me."

"You don't understand, feller," Hugo said quickly. "We'll be backin' you up, all right. Just let Higley, or anybody else, try to take you away from here. We're all in this thing too deep to throw down a pal. I wa'n't meanin' to doubt your word, Manitoba, only I wanted to get all the facts clear in my mind. I'm believin' every word you said. Hell! Why wouldn't I?"

"Yeah, why in hell wouldn't you?" Manitoba snapped. "You better stick to me, 'cause it looks like hell would break loose around here before long. Them two fellers ridin' with Madigan, when I first see him yesterday mornin', was headin' for the Rafter-S."

Squint Cantrell nodded. "I see 'em ride in when I was spyin' on that outfit, like Hugo ordered. And there was two other hombres there, too. I wa'n't close enough to recognize any of 'em, but I'll bet a mess of hop-toads that Madigan borrowed 'em from the Slash-O and Lazy-V, just like you heard him talkin' it over with Jug-Handle, Hugo. And that Jug-Handle hobo is ridin' for the Rafter-S, too."

"We got a fight ahead, all right," Hugo nodded, "but I'll get the Rafter-S, if it's the last thing I do. We'll raid 'em some night when they least expect it, then we'll see how much chance Norris will have to pay off that mortgage. I gotta have water, that's all. And I'll get the remainder of his stock, too."

"Trouble is," Guy Du Sang put in, "you didn't go about things right, Hugo. You should have let me go visitin' that daughter of Norris'. Once she got sweet on me, you could do just about what you want."

Hugo scowled. "Dammit, Guy, I've told you a hundred times that gal ain't your kind. She's the sort that wants to marry the feller she gets stuck on. Trouble with you is, you think every woman you look at is goin' to get mashed on you."

"We could'a' fixed up a fake marriage of some kind—" Guy commenced.

"You make me tired," Hugo snapped. "I ain't got no morals when it comes to fightin' men, but I ain't never yet descended to pullin' a dirty trick like that on a gal, and I don't intend to start now. That's just the sort of thing that'd turn the whole country against us, and the last few days we ain't been so popular in Vaca Wells. You just leave matters to me, and we'll come out on top of the heap. The first thing we gotta do is get rid of Madigan. After that, things will commence runnin' on the old tracks again."

"I'll get rid of Madigan, myself," Manitoba announced abruptly. "This outfit has stood just about enough from that red-headed——"

"Yaah!" Guy Du Sang spat scornfully. "How you goin' to do it, Manitoba? You're great at runnin' off at the mouth about what you're goin' to do, but that's as far as it goes. You've had two chances and you flopped both times——"

"You didn't show up so good, yourself," Manitoba flared. "You and Luke both must 'a' been asleep to let that waddy run ragged over you the way he did."

Guy's face crimsoned. "I pulled my iron on him, any-how, which is more than you can say, the first day you'n him met——"

"Yeah, and if you'd had my speed, you'd have got him," Manitoba retorted hotly. "Damn you, Guy. I'll——" He leaped from his seat and started around the table.

Hugo jumped to his feet and pushed Manitoba back. "A fine pair you two are," he growled, "to start a fight at a time like this, when I need every man. Sit down! Keep your traps shut, do you hear? I'm runnin' this spread, and don't you two forget it. I'm doin' the thinkin' for the outfit, too. When there's fightin' to be done, I'll let you know. Think that over."

Guy and Manitoba subsided into a sullen silence. The rest of the crew finished breakfast with little conversation. Chairs were pushed back, there came a scraping of booted feet, and the men filed outside. Singly, and in twos, they crossed the ranch yard toward the bunkhouse. A couple of the hands entered the building, and reappeared in a minute to flop down on the long bench outside the door. The others gathered around, some on the bench, some squatting on their heels before the others.

The Chinese cook appeared with an old tin beer tray upon which he carried Luke's breakfast. He gave it into Hugo's hands. Guy accompanied Hugo up to the ranch

125

house. Halfway there. Hugo turned and called to the group in front of the bunkhouse, "I'll outline the day's work when I come back. Meanwhile, you hombres see that your guns is in workin' order, in case we decide to go visitin'."

This caused much speculation and considerable conversation. Two of the men who had not yet buckled on their guns, entered the bunkhouse to get them. One man procured oil and rags and proceeded to clean his forty-five.

An hour passed while the sun climbed higher above the eastern horizon. Hugo and Guy, by this time, had joined the others before the bunkhouse.

"I was kinda thinkin' mebbe we'd call on Norris," Hugo commenced, "but on second thought that can wait. We gotta get Madigan outta the way, first. I wish I could think of a way to get him separated from his crew. I might send him word that he's skeered to meet me in Vaca Wells and shoot it out——"

"Somebody comin'," Hub Wheeler announced suddenly. His pointing arm directed attention to a scurrying cloud of dust that moved rapidly along the trail that led to town.

"An' comin' plumb fast," Calico Worden added.

Hugo raised one hand to shield his eyes from the rays of the early morning sun, looked steadily at the approaching horseman. Finally, he lowered his arm. "Doc Kenyon ain't due out here until this afternoon, so it can't be him. He wouldn't be ridin' like that, anyway. He knows Luke ain't in no danger. I can't think of only one man it might be, and that's Big-Foot Higley. Mebbe Higley's got his nerve back, and is comin' to square hisself with me. Damn his hide. I'll give him what-for, when he gets here. Yeller coyote! I can stand anythin' but a hombre that ain't got guts."

"That may be Higley," Tate Munson pointed out, "but I doubt it. Higley ain't got no hawss that'll rip off miles thataway, and he can't ride like that hombre, neither. 'Tain't Higley."

"Naw, that ain't Higley," Calico Worden agreed a minute later. "Different build from Higley."

The men watched the approaching rider with interest. He came nearer. Suddenly, a curse was torn from Guy Du Sang's lips. "Madigan!" he explained. "That's who 'tis—Madigan!"

126

"By Gawd, you're right!" Manitoba burst out a minute later. "Wonder what he wants."

"I dunno, and I don't give a damn!" Guy grated. "I only know what I'm goin' to do when he gets here." He reached his left hand to holster and procured his Colt-gun.

Manitoba was quick to catch the idea. He, too, drew his six-shooter. "Guy, you lay off," he warned. "That Madigan hombre is my meat."

"You'll both put them hawg-laigs away!" Hugo roared. "I want to see what Madigan wants. Go on, put 'em away, before I bust you over the conk!"

Reluctantly, the two sheathed their weapons, although Manitoba's hand hovered near his holster, ready for a quick draw. He was commencing to suspect, now, the reason that brought Madigan to the Diamond-8. "Damn him!" he grated. "I bet he's guessed that I killed Pee-Wee, and he's comin' to see whether I'll admit it."

Hugo nodded quickly. "You're probably right. Well, we'll bluff him out. Tell him we don't know nothin' about that. After——"

He didn't finish the sentence, but the very silence held a meaning for the men. No one spoke for several minutes. Without checking his pony in the slightest, Madigan swept the sure-footed little beast around the turn in the road and came plunging into the ranch yard.

The men got to their feet as he approached, prepared to scatter. For a moment it loked as though he intended to run them down. Suddenly, he jerked the sweat-streaked, foam-flecked Jezebel back to haunches, some fifteen feet from the waiting crew.

"You wantin' somethin', Madigan?" Hugo demanded, as Melody made no move to dismount.

Melody's gaze rested a moment on Du Sang, then swiftly ran over the others until it came to Manitoba. There it stopped, his eyes narrowed to thin slits. For the first time he spoke.

"I thought a heap of Pee-Wee, Manitoba," he said.

His voice was flat, emotionless, though it carried a deadly quality the others weren't missing. They stared at him without sound, something of awe creeping into their faces as they noticed how Manitoba seemed to shrivel before the red anger that burned in Melody's narrowed eyes.

Stark fear had entered Manitoba's heart. He remembered

127

the first day he met Madigan, the prickly sensation that had coursed his spine, lifting the hair at the back of his neck. The man opened his mouth to shout denial of his guilt, but the words wouldn't come. He realized, now, that denial would be useless. Finally, his gaze dropped before Madigan's.

The others stood like granite statues. For all the attention Melody paid them, they might not have been there. He slipped quickly from his horse, and advanced two paces nearer Manitoba.

Something pleading in his voice, now: "Ain't you ever goin' to fill your hand, Manitoba? I'm givin' you more chance than you give Pee-Wee. You got your guns. His was loaned, and you *knew* he didn't have none."

Manitoba couldn't answer.

Silence, save for the strained breathing of the men. Melody's eyes blazed like furies incarnate, but his voice came strangely steady, "Look at me, snake. I'm givin' you your chance."

Suddenly, he threw both arms high in the air, and for the first time his pent up rage burst forth. "Damn you, Manitoba, draw your irons!"

Manitoba raised his eyes, and could scarcely believe the sight they beheld—Madigan, standing near, hands well above his head!

Like a cornered rat, Manitoba moved into action, reached to holsters. Maybe fright slowed his movements; something prevented his usual, swift shooting.

His talon-like claws had not yet touched gun-butts, when Madigan's hands swooped down. The guns in his holsters seemed to leap to meet his eager palms. The two guns streaked up—out! Melody commenced thumbing lead out of his guns in instant the muzzles cleared leather!

Two slugs kicked up the dust at Manitoba's feet, before the twin barrels cut swift arcs upward to find Manitoba's range. The next shots found his body—and so the next!

Guns half out of holsters, Manitoba paused abruptly. Then, he completed the draw, but it came too late. His form stiffened, pulling him to tip-toes. He turned half around, then pitched forward in a huddled heap on the earth, convulsive muscular action working triggers and sending shot after shot ripping harmlessly across the ranch yard!

Quite suddenly Manitoba's fingers ceased moving and

he lay still. A look of grim satisfaction flitted across Melody's face. For the first time he seemed to realize the presence of the other Diamond-8 men. He backed slowly toward his horse, guns covering Hugo and the rest. His voice came through the smoke that curled from their muzzles.

"I thought a heap of Pee-Wee," he said again.

The others appeared too stunned by the outcome of the shooting to reach for their forty-fives, or even to speak.

Hugo finally found his voice, "We didn't know it was that way, Madigan," he said slowly. "Manitoba told us it was a fair fight. Go on, kid, climb on your bronc. Nobody's goin' to throw down on you. Me, I can stand anythin' but a hombre without guts, and you got plenty! I recognize nerve when I see it, and you deserve a square deal. I'd like to shake your hand, but I know you wouldn't do it."

"I couldn't, Du Sang," Melody said steadily. "You'n me don't ride the same sort of a range—an' that means war. Howsomever, I'm recognizin' what you're doin' and I'm appreciatin' it.'

"That's whatever," Du Sang stated coldly. "Next time we meet, start smokin' your guns. You won't get a second chance."

Melody nodded shortly, turned his back on the group, climbed to the saddle. "You can't come shootin' too fast to suit me, Du Sang," he challenged.

Without another word, he wheeled Jezebel, and loped her out of the yard. The instant his back was turned, Guy Du Sang reached to holster. With an angry oath, Hugo leaped to his brother's side, wrested the gun from Guy's grasp.

"You fool!" Guy raged. "You've made us miss the best chance we'll ever get at that hombre."

Hugo didn't answer for a moment. None of the others had made an attempt to draw. He glanced down at the lifeless body of Manitoba, and Hugo's lip curled with contempt. Then his eyes strayed to the swiftly-moving rider, ripping plumes of dust from the trail.

After a time, Hugo Du Sang gave a short affirmative nod. "I reckon you're right, Guy," he admitted a trifle sheepishly. "We've missed the best chance we ever had at Madigan."

The men looked at him in wonder. It was unusual to see their chief back down in such manner.

Guy Du Sang said sarcastically. "What's the matter, you contracted a yellow streak, Hugo?"

Hugo slowly shook his head. "You know damn well that's not the case. You see, somehow, I just couldn't help admirin' his nerve. He deserved a clean break——"

"Yaah!" Guy said with some disgust. "You'll be shinin' his boots, next, if you go on this way. Why don't you ride over to the Rafter-S? If you're humble enough, mebbe he'll give you a job——"

"That's enough of that, Guy!" Hugo thundered, his face suddenly crimson. "You know damn well I ain't changed in my idees. Things go through as planned. Madigan's got to be put out of the way. But we got to settle down to business right quick, before I get to likin' that red-headed devil too much. I only wish you hombres had one-tenth of his nerve. You can say what you want—he's a man, from the top of his sorrel thatch down to his spurs—more of a man than any of you will ever be—nor me, neither, I reckon."

The Diamond-8 crew stood speechless a moment, hardly knowing what to say. Guy Du Sang started to speak, but could only choke with anger at thought of the manner in which Madigan had escaped his wrath.

Finally, Calico Worden found his tongue, "Well, if that's the way you feel——" he commenced in disgruntled tones.

"That's the way I feel," Hugo flared suddenly, "exactly the way I feel, but I ain't asked nobody's opinion. What you all standin' around like a bunch of dummies for?" Suddenly ashamed at his display of inner feelings of a few minutes before he loosed on his men such a torrent of cursing that they turned away in awe.

"——yes, that's the way I feel," he concluded, voice trembling with rage. Jerking one thumb toward the dead body of Manitoba, he went on, "Get that carcass out of here. Take it away, bury it. Do somethin'. An' thank your Gawd that the lousy yellow buzzard won't be livin' with you no longer. There ain't no place on the Diamond-8 for cowardly skunks!"

# 20. Jug-Handle Gets Evidence

TEN DAYS slipped quickly past. Under Melody's capable supervision the Rafter-S was fast getting back to normal. His first move had been to put Oliver and Clem Osborne to work branding all the unmarked stock that could be found in the valley. Though Norris wasn't yet able to ride a horse, he did his part in tending the branding irons and having ever ready to hand one of the new stamp-irons, heated to a cherry red.

While this was going on, Melody, Jug-Handle, Tennessee Lee and Mesquite Farrell were combing the hills and ravines west and north of the Rafter-S ranch buildings. The draws of the rugged Trozar Mountains were particularly productive. Here were found, and driven from cover, a considerable number of stock that had strayed away, or been overlooked during round-ups of past seasons.

Some of these renegades hadn't seen a man, nor horse, for some years and were pretty wild, though most of the older animals had been branded with the Rafter-S mark at some time or other. Each night the punchers rode in, driving before them small bunches of cows—four-year olds, long threes, some twos, and a large number of yearlings. These, the following day were turned into the branding chutes and felt the heat of Oliver's and Osborne's stamp irons, Norris taking a hand at the work with renewed hope.

The days since the shooting of Manitoba hadn't carried any events of great interest. Pee-Wee Page had been buried in the Vaca Wells cemetery, and his funeral had been attended by nearly everyone for miles around. The town had awakened the morning after the funeral to discover that Sheriff Big-Foot Higley had left a note of resignation on his desk and abruptly departed from Vaca Wells. Undoubtedly, Higley had read the writing on the wall and had decided to travel while traveling was safe.

For the time being, the town was deprived of a law officer, and Melody expected every day to see the Diamond-8 outfit break loose with further villainies, but nothing of the sort took place. Evidently, Hugo Du Sang was biding his time.

Meanwhile, the herd of cows in the Rafter-S valley was rapidly assuming favorable proportions. Expecting daily to have their tasks interrupted by the machinations of Du Sang, the men worked doubly hard that they might be prepared when the break for action came, and the work went forward with scarcely a hitch.

Jerry acted as cook for the outfit. As the days passed, fewer cattle were brought in, and Tom Norris sometimes helped the girl in the kitchen. Several times, Jerry had doffed her green-checked gingham dress to put on overalls and take short rides with Melody, ostensibly to help him drive stray stock out of the brush. The two were seeing considerable of each other these days. Jerry was deciding that the cowboy wore well. As for Melody, well, he'd fallen into a habit of blushing every time the girl's name was mentioned in his presence. All of which was rather unusual for Melody.

At the conclusion of dinner one noon, Norris asked, "What's to do this afternoon, Melody? We finished burnin' the last dang cow this mornin'. Wa'n't many brung in yesterday, you recollect."

Melody nodded, setting down his empty coffee cup. "Looks like we been over this range with a fine-tooth comb. Howsomever, I aim to ride a mite this afternoon, to make sure we ain't missed any cows."

"What's for the rest of us?" Tennessee Lee asked.

Melody's eyes glanced around the table, rested fondly a moment on Jerry, then stopped at Jug-Handle. "Jug-Handle will ride with me," Melody announced. "Matt Oliver can cover the range to the north. We're nearly out of supplies. Clem, you hitch up the wagon and go into Vaca Wells for 'em. Tom made up a list of what's needed, this mornin'. . . . Mesquite, you and Tenn better stick around here. There's white-wash in the barn." Melody smiled, "You two can turn artist for a spell. There's buildin's and so on that will stand a mite of fixin' up an' repairin'. When you get that finished——"

"Danged if you ain't a slave driver," Tenneeess Lee groaned. "You don't want some post-holes dug for a new corral, nor nothin' do you, when we finish them light jobs——"

"That *is* an idea," Melody said promptly. "Thanks for remindin' me, Tenn——"

"Tennessee Lee," Mesquite Farrell spoke disgustedly, "you keep your mouth shut from now to henceforth. Ain't you got no brains, a-tall? Gettin' us all that extra work."

A series of smiles passed around the table, in which Lee and Farrell ruefully joined. Jerry said, "Melody, would I be in the way if I rode with you and Jug-Handle this afternoon?"

"Not a bit of it," Melody grinned. "We'll be glad to have you with us—providin' Tom can spare you——"

"You go ahead, girl," Tom Norris broke in. "I'll wash these dinner dishes and red up the kitchen while you're gone. Don't hurry none. I'll get supper started."

"Reckon I'll change to riding things, then," Jerry smiled, rising from the table. "Melody, will you saddle up for me, while you're waiting?"

"Surest thing you know."

The men rose from their chairs and sauntered outside, rolling cigarettes. Osborne and Oliver finished their smokes and went about their respective duties: Oliver to saddle up and ride north in search of strays; Osborne to hitch up the team for the trip into town. Melody and Jug-Handle were mounted, five minutes later, and waiting for the girl when she emerged from the house. Melody got down and handed over the reins of Jerry's horse when she had climbed to the saddle. Then, he, too, got up, settled his feet to the stirrups. The three moved off.

"We headin' west?" Jug-Handle looked at Melody. A change had come over the tramp since he'd been working at the Rafter-S. From some place—no one had inquired where—he had produced range togs. Now, he looked every inch the cowman, from the crown of his rolled-brim buckskin-colored sombrero, down to his big-roweled spurs. It was plain at a glance that he had been born to the saddle. Of his roping ability, there wasn't the slightest doubt. That had been too often put to the test the past ten days to deny the fact. Melody stated frankly that there wasn't a man on the Rafter-S that could approach Jug-Handle, when it came to a matter of "dabbin' a string on a cow critter."

"West it is," Melody nodded reply to Jug-Handle's words. "I doubt if there's any cows left in the foothills of the Trozars, but I'd like to see, before I take the next step."

"Next step?" from Jerry. She was riding between the two men.

Melody explained. "I figure to take a trip to the capital and see if I can locate a cattle-buyer with ready money. We'll ship early this year. Now that we got all those cows bunched in the valley, there ain't no use lettin' 'em scatter, again. They'll stay near the stream—leastwise until their brands are healed."

Jerry sighed happily. "You've sure done something, cowboy."

The horses had cut through the cottonwoods surrounding the ranch buildings and were ascending a long, gradual slope of grassy terrain. Melody wheeled momentarily to glance back along the valley floor. As far as his gaze reached he saw slowly moving reddish-brown backs—the ten days' gathering of Hereford cows.

The look of pride in his face when he again settled to his saddle, was pardonable. Melody *had* done something, and he knew it. But he wasn't ready to admit the fact, yet. There was still more to be done.

"Done somethin'?" he grinned disparagingly. "Shucks! You ain't seen nothin', yet. Biggest job I've done so far is gettin' Jug-Handle to take up work. Ain't that right, feller?"

Jug-Handle laughed, but made no reply. He was strangely quiet, as though trying to solve some knotty problem in his mind, or decide on his next move.

The horses pounded on in a long ground-devouring lope. Conversation languished. It was difficult to make themselves understood in the swift rush of wind that whipped past their cheeks. The Trozar Range drew nearer after a time, its jagged peaks standing out in clear sharp lines against the turquoise sky. Another half hour passed with the horses veering toward the south. As yet, no stray cows had been seen, though in this open country that was to be expected. Better luck might be encountered when they got into the deep slashes and brushy ravines of the Trozars.

Jug-Handle suddenly called for a halt. Melody and the girl drew their ponies to a stop.

134

"Did you have any particular spot in mind, you was headin' for, Melody?" Jug-Handle asked.

Melody shook his head. "Why, what you got on your mind?"

Jug-Handle smiled quizzically at the two. "You ain't no objections to me pullin' away, and lettin' you two go on alone, have you?"

Melody flushed crimson. He'd been wishing for some such arrangement, but didn't like to suggest it. Jerry busied herself, tucking a stray tendril of red-gold hair under her Stetson. Both Melody and the girl tried to appear nonchalant. And didn't succeed very well in the attempt.

"What you got in mind?" Melody asked.

"Sort of figured to look over on that south range a mite," Jug-Handle explained.

Melody stiffened slightly. "That's gettin' right close to Diamond-8 holdin's," he reminded.

"I know that. I don't figure to go far——"

"You aimin' to go see Du Sang?"

Jug-Handle shook his head. "Nope, I ain't ready to see Du Sang—not yet. And not alone."

"You got somethin' on your mind," Melody accused.

"Reckon I have," Jug-Handle admitted.

He didn't say what it was, nor did Melody inquire.

Melody nodded at last. "Sure, go ahead. But don't run any chances of a ruckus with the Du Sangs."

Jug-Handle smiled, bathering up his reins. "Not me. I don't like fightin' no more than I do work."

"Judgin' from that," Melody grinned, "I'd like to have you at my back in a ruckus. I've seen you work, remember."

"*Adios.*" Jug-Handle touched fingers to the brim of his sombrero, wheeled the horse and headed due south.

"There," Jerry said quietly, "goes the strangest acting tramp I ever laid eyes on."

"If he ever was a tramp," Melody replied, "I'm Santa Claus. I wonder what he's got in mind. He seemed anxious to leave us."

Impulsively, Jerry said, "I wonder if he thought he was intruding——" She stopped abruptly, crimson creeping into her cheeks.

Melody frowned. "Huh, how could he be——"

Jerry put spurs to her pony's sides. "Come on," she

135

called back over her shoulder, "I'll race you to that tall clump of prickly-pear ahead."

In an instant, Melody was after her. By the time they had reached the end of the race, both forgot what they'd been talking about.

Jug-Handle pushed steadily on for the next hour. By that time he had left Rafter-S grazing lands and was trespassing on Diamond-8 territory. He pulled the horse to a walk, now, and advanced more cautiously, his senses alert for the first sign of a Diamond-8 puncher.

Here it was all rolling country. Before reaching the top of each rise, Jug-Handle dismounted and went forward on foot to learn what lay ahead of him. Then, he'd mount and ride on. He was commencing to see straggling bunches of Diamond-8 cows, now. Whenever he passed any of the animals, he slowed his horse and looked their brands over thoroughly. Many of the brands looked fresh, a few were just commencing to peel. Others were considerably older and haired-over.

"Sort of looks like," Jug-Handle muttered to himself, "the Du Sangs had been combin' this territory, too, so they could grab off stock before we come to it. Some of these cows, wearin' the Diamond-8, has been burned quite recent. Ten to one Du Sang has had spies out, watchin' our activities."

He rode on, straight toward the southeast for another fifteen minutes. Finally, he pulled to a halt, frowning.

"Reckon I better not go into Diamond-8 territory any farther," he mused. "Another half hour's ride would bring me to the Du Sang ranch house, and I ain't hankerin' to get that close." His frown deepened, "It's dang funny I ain't seen nobody. Wonder where all Du Sang's hands are? I ain't seen hide nor hair of a rider. Well, I reckon I better get busy, and not waste no more time."

He wheeled the pony, touched spurs to its sides, and rapidly headed back in the direction from which he'd come. After a half hour's loping across the range, the bunches of cows he'd been seeing, commenced to thin out. Finally, off to the right a short distance he picked out three Diamond-8 cows.

As his horse started toward the animals, they left off their grazing and began to edge rapidly away. Jug-Handle's pony quickly closed the distance between itself and the cows. The Herefords were in full flight, now.

Jug-Handle reached for the rope on his saddle and commenced shaking out a loop. A few minutes later, he was close enough to distinguish the Du Sang brand on their hairy ribs. Singling out the nearest white-face, Jug-Handle commenced to swing his rope.

The little cow-pony was quick to understand which animal its rider wished to separate from the others. Now, two of the cows had swerved to one side. The cow-pony was close on the heels of the third cow. There came the swift staccato drumming of hoofs as the pony carried its rider near enough for an easy throw.

The rope left Jug-Handle's hand, sailed through the air, and settled surely over the cow's head. The pony stopped, settled back to haunches. The rope tightened, went taut. In a cloud of dust, the cow crashed to the earth.

In an instant, Jug-Handle was out of the saddle and running down the straining rope. The cow was on its side, struggling to arise, as the pony backed slowly away to prevent such action. Jug-Handle cast one quick glance at the Diamond-8 brand, then drew his six-shooter.

The report of the gun echoed flatly across the hills, the cow quivered a moment, then lay still. Jug-Handle bent over the brand on the cow's side. Drawing his Barlow knife and opening it, he made four quick slashes encircling the brand. After that it was a matter of minutes and deft, sure strokes, to skin out the brand.

A moment later, he straightened from the dead cow's side, holding the wet section of hide with its Diamond-8 brand. He glanced at both sides for an instant, then rolled up the hide, hairy side out. With the rolled hide under his arm, he hurried to the pony and mounted. The lariat grew taut once more, then the pony moved off, dragging the dead carcass at the end of the rope.

Again, in the saddle, Jug-Handle scanned the horizon in all directions. His features knit to a look of perplexity. "Dam'd if I understand it. There just don't seem to be no Diamond-8 hands in this vicinity. That shot should have brought anyone in hearin' distance. Somethin' queer about this. I wonder what Du Sang's cookin' up, now."

He rode on. At the end of twenty minutes they had reached a dry arroyo. Down into the arroyo, Jug-Handle guided the pony, dragging the dead cow behind him. In a short time he had come to a low mesquite tree which hung over the edge of the ancient stream bed. Beneath the thorny branches of the mesquite, Jug-Handle loosened and coiled his rope.

He glanced down at the dead body of the cow. "Reckon this is as good a place as any to leave this carcass. I ain't keen on havin' Du Sang find it—leastwise, not right away. Don't want him to know what we've done—not until I've got my cards all dealt for playin'."

He climbed back to the saddle, and headed the cow-pony up to level ground again. Then, he rode off in the direction of the Rafter-S outfit.

A mile distant, he turned once and glanced back from the saddle. High above the point where he had left the dead cow, a buzzard wheeled and soared on motionless wings. An instant later, the bird swooped down and disappeared from sight.

"Leave it to them buzzards to smell death," he mused, then added, "I wonder just how many more of them scavengers is due to head this way, before this range is cleared of skunks and killers."

Settling once more to the saddle, he pressed his pony forward at a faster pace.

# 21. Important Business

For Melody and Jerry it had been an enjoyable afternoon. They hadn't been able to scare up a single stray cow in their ride, but the time had passed swiftly—all too swiftly to suit either of them. The sun had already dipped behind the highest peaks of the Trozars and the homeward-bound horses threw long shadows ahead of them.

Neither the man, nor girl, took any heed of the passage of time. Their mounts had slowed to a walk, without either rider noticing the change of gait. Melody's heart was full of the things he wanted to say, but he didn't know just how to start. And then, it happened, before Melody, or Jerry, realized what was taking place.

The two had dipped down into a hollow that lay about three miles back of the Rafter-S ranch house. Melody had dismounted to tighten his cinch which had worked loose. The girl had also stepped to the ground and stood near, watching him.

Melody straightened from the horse, turned to the girl. In that instant, something took place within the breasts of both. Jerry's hat was off, and the setting sun was picking out touches of gold in her finely spun hair. The bronze highlights caught Melody's eyes for a moment, drew him on. He stepped forward, then checked himself, his gaze dropping a bit to meet Jerry's. Quite suddenly, he realized her arms were lifting to him.

His own arms went around the girl. For minutes neither spoke. Words weren't necessary at a time like this. Their heads came closer together, as his lips met the girl's. A long long silence . . . and the sunshine . . . and a breeze bringing a faint scent of sage to the nostrils. . . .

The two horses strayed off a short distance and commenced to crop grass. Neither man nor girl noticed them. The world had ceased revolving and all things seemed to stand still in the consummation of that happy moment.

Her face flushed, Jerry finally released herself from his arms. Melody found his tongue, "Oh, gee-gosh," he exclaimed happily, "I didn't know you felt that way, too. It all come on so sudden. I can't hardly believe it's true——"

The girl's lips lightly brushed his own. "Cowboy," she laughed softly, dropping into range vernacular, "ain't you always said us red-heads has got to stick together? Me, I'm takin' you at your word."

Melody eyed her in silence, scarcely believing the incredible wonder of it all. Then he grinned. "C'mon," he drawled, "let's do it some more. I've just discovered that you're plumb kissable."

And she was, too.

It was some time later that he caught up the horses. They mounted and finished the journey to the Rafter-S, riding slowly, stirrup to stirrup.

Tom Norris and his men were just sitting down to supper when Melody and the girl arrived at the ranch house. All were there, except Clem Osborne, who hadn't as yet returned from his trip to town for supplies. Jug-Handle glanced up at Jerry and Melody. A cryptic smile crossed his countenance, but he said nothing.

Jerry and Melody took their places at the table. Tom Norris looked at the two for a few seconds, then chuckled, "I was kinda worryin' when you two didn't arrive," he said, "but I can see, now, that I just wasted my time."

Melody crammed a forkful of food into his mouth. "We had important business," he announced.

"Awfully important," Jerry added steadily. Her cheeks were tinged with pink as she said the words.

Tom Norris' leathery face crinkled to a grin. He glanced at the smiling faces of the men, then back to his daughter and Melody. "We all been sorta wonderin' when you two would decide," he laughed. "We could see it comin' on you younkers, day by day." He rounded the table, hand outstretched to Melody, "Congrats, son, I don't know nobody I'd sooner see marry Jerry."

Melody stood up and seized the proffered hand. "I'm statin' to the world in general," he smiled happily, "that I'm one lucky cowpoke!"

The other men burst into cheers. "Goin' to have a weddin', goin' to have a weddin', going to have a weddin' mighty soon," Mesquite Farrell sang loudly. They all crowded around to shake hands with Melody and the girl.

In the midst of the uproar, Clem Osborne arrived. He gave vent to a wild cowboy yell when he learned the news, and swung around to Tennessee Lee, "you can pay me, Tenn," he exclaimed. "I win."

"Reckon you-all do," Lee admitted sheepishly. He put his hand in his pocket and drew out some money which he passed across to Osborne.

"What's all the bettin' about?" Melody queried.

Osborne explained. "Me'n Tennessee been makin' a bet on how long you two would hold out," he told Jerry and Melody. "Tenn said you wouldn't come to no arrangement until after the trouble with the Diamond-8 was over. I been allowin' you two kids couldn't wait that long. You see, I was a youngster once, myself, and I know. Tenn, here, he's still a youngster and ain't got the mellow wisdom that comes with years."

"He ain't got no wisdom a-tall," Mesquite Farrell wailed. "Part of them bucks he lost was mine. I told him not to make no such bets."

" 'S'all right, Mesquite," Matt Oliver grinned complacently. "Clem was bettin' my money along with his own. I happen to be on the winnin' end while you're on the losin', that's all. That's the only difference between you'n me."

Jug-Handle laughed softly. "There's two things what nobody can't ever dope out," he said, "an' therefore makes plumb risky objects to bet on."

"What's that?" Jerry wanted to know.

"A cowpunch that's in love," Jug-Handle answered.

"You said *two* things," Melody reminded. "What's the other?"

"The girl he's in love with, of course," Jug-Handle replied.

The laughter died down after a time, and Clem Osborne gave the group the news while he ate his supper. The others sat at the table in the kitchen of the ranch house, smoking cigarettes and listening.

"There's been an upheaval on the Diamond-8," Osborne announced. "Just before I pulled outta Vaca Wells, the whole crew rode in. They allowed as they was sick of workin' for the Du Sang brothers and had quit in a body."

"That leaves the Du Sangs there alone, don't it?" Mesquite Farrell asked. "Shucks! I was hopin' we'd be able to

141

ride over there one of these days and trade some lead with that outfit."

Tom Norris considered. "Looks like Hugo Du Sang's men was gettin' cold feet."

Melody said nothing except, "Du Sang is due for a reckonin' right soon. Seems like the sun is commencin' to shine on our range for a change."

The matter was discussed for some time, then Osborne released his second piece of news. "Melody," he asked, "what you aimin' to do with that saloon Pee-Wee left you?"

Melody frowned. "Danged if I know," he replied slowly. "I ain't got no hankerin' to run a bar."

"Oh, Lord," groaned Mesquite Farrell, "he owns a saloon and don't know what to do with it." He turned to Tennessee with mock seriousness, "Think of it, Tenn. He owns plenty liquor, an' ——"

"Where you're concerned, Mesquite," Lee drawled, "they ain't no such thing as *plenty* liquor."

"Aw-w," Mesquite protested, red-faced. "I don't drink as much as you do, you slab-sided, cow-hocked excuse for a cow-nurse."

"Yes," Jerry laughed, "you two boys are terrible drunkards, aren't you? To hear you talk, a person would think you were both prime to take the cure, or something. As a matter of fact, I don't think either of you has had a drink since you've been on the Rafter-S."

"That's true," Matt Oliver said darkly, "an' somethin' ought to be done about it before Tenn and Mesquite run amuck. When they get that turrible cravin' for sarsaprilly water, there ain't no controllin' 'em."

"Mebbe the Here's A Go should be opened again," Melody continued, when the laughter had subsided, "but I'm darned if I can see my way clear to doin' it. Why you askin', Clem?"

"Talked to a feller in Vaca Wells, today," Osborne explained. "He's a newcomer in town and is lookin' for a location to open a saloon. Seems like a square shooter. He was askin' about the Here's A Go, and is willin' to pay cash. I told him I'd tell you, and you could ride in and talk to him."

Melody considered. "Not a bad idea, at that," he nodded after a time. "Tom has suggested a partnership to me, and I could use the money to pay for——"

"You've more than paid, Melody, for any share you get in the Rafter-S," Norris broke in.

"Well, we'll give it a thought later," Melody concluded. "I think if Pee-Wee was alive, he'd take to the idea."

The talk turned to ranch matters. Matt Oliver had brought in two strays that day; the others had returned empty-handed. "I reckon we've covered the range pretty thorough," Melody said. "An' we've built a nice little herd in the valley. Now that we know what you got, Tom, I want to look at your tally book, and see just what's been rustled. Then we can put certain propositions up to the Diamond-8."

Jug-Handle had left the room and gone outside while the men talked. Now he returned, bearing in one hand the roll of green cowhide he'd skinned from the cow that afternoon.

"Osborne bringin' news about the Diamond-8 crew quittin'," he commenced, "explains why I didn't see no riders on that range today———"

Melody's eyes widened a trifle. "Were you ridin' the Du Sang holdin's, after you left Jerry and me?" he demanded in surprise.

Jug-Handle nodded. "Yeah, lookin' over their stock a mite. When I found a cow that looked likely, I shot it and skinned out the brand. Give a look at this."

Dishes were pushed back. Jug-Handle unrolled the portion of hide and exposed the hairy side to the gaze of the group about the table. "To all appearances," he said, "this is from a Diamond-8 cow. As a matter of fact, that's a blotted brand. It used to be a Rafter-S."

He turned the piece of hide over to show the inner side. There, as plain as day, could be seen the original Rafter-S brand, with the Diamond-8 design joining it. The underside of the hide told the story, as it showed clearly where the lines of the bogus brand joined the old.

"There's your evidence," Jug-Handle said simply. Due to Jerry's presence, the men checked the oaths that rose to their lips.

" 'Course we all been sure that Du Sang was stealin' our cows," Jug-Handle continued, "but we needed actual proof to produce in court."

"And you had plenty nerve," Melody said admiringly, "to ride over on Diamond-8 range and shoot a cow that was supposed to belong to that outfit."

"Aw, that wa'n't nothin'," Jug-Handle protested. "You see, none of the crew was ridin' today. As Osborne told you, they'd quit."

"But you didn't know that when you went over there," Melody pointed out. "You got a vote of thanks comin' to you."

"Dang it all," Tom Norris said, "Sheriff Higley leavin' town, like he did, sorta puts us in a hole. If he was on the job, we could make him ride over and put this matter up to Du Sang. Seems to me the county oughta get busy and elect another sheriff."

Jug-Handle laughed shortly. "I reckon we don't need to worry about gettin' authority to handle Du Sang," he said. "There ain't no use of me keepin' it secret any longer. My name's Jugandel, and I'm an operative for the Artexico Cattlemen's Association. I think Melody has been suspecting me right along."

"Well, I'll be everlastingly goldarned!" Tom Norris exploded. "A cattle detective! Thought it was danged funny the Association didn't send another man down, when that last one got killed."

Similar exclamations of surprise echoed through the room. "Gosh!" Melody said after a time, "it's goin' to be danged hard to give up callin' you Jug-Handle, now that we got used to that name."

"It fits all right," Jugandel replied. "Nickname of mine. I figured it would be good to use when I come down here in that tramp disguise. I'm hopin' before this business is finished, to get Du Sang to admit that the Diamond-8 was responsible for the death of our other operative."

"So long as you're the law around here," Norris said, "I'm cravin' to know when you aim to move on the Diamond-8 and get things settled."

"With this piece of hide for evidence," Jugandel replied, "there ain't any use of us waitin' no longer. I figure we'll all ride over to the Diamond-8 in the morning. Then I'll arrest the three Du Sangs, and we'll get the law to workin' on 'em."

"Shucks!" from Mesquite Farrell. "I was hopin' there'd be a fight. Darn you dyspeptics—I mean detectives—anyhow. You spoil all the fun."

The men gradually arose from the table and drifted down to the bunkhouse. Only Jugandel, Melody, Norris and Jerry remained in the kitchen.

144

At Melody's request, Norris produced the Rafter-S tally book. While the three men were looking over its pages, Jerry commenced washing the dishes.

From time to time, Melody jotted down lead pencil figures on a sheet of writing-tablet paper. Once he asked Norris the amount still due on the Rafter-S mortgage. Norris gave it to him.

Finally, Melody after considerable calculating, raised his head from the figures before him. "It looks to me, Tom," he said, "as though your mortgage would have been paid up by this time, if Du Sang hadn't been stealin' you blind."

"My idea exact," Norris agreed.

"Did you figure the normal stock losses?" Jugandel asked.

Melody nodded. "Figured a certain loss for each year, and the natural percentage of increase, too. I got a pretty fair idea of what beef has been bringin' the past few seasons. I even deducted the wages Tom would have paid out, if he'd had a full crew working for him right along, and any way you look at it, there should have been enough money come in to have paid off that mortgage."

"Well, we'll settle with Du Sang tomorrow mornin'," Jugandel promised.

"I forgot to mention it before," Norris put in, "but George Vaughn and Buck Kirby rode over to see me, today."

"Wantin' anythin' in particular?" Melody asked.

Norris shook his head. "Mostly, they said they come to apologize for not gettin' in touch with me long before this. Said if I wanted any more men, I could have 'em. Darn nice hombres, both of 'em. I was just wonderin' if mebbe we oughta get a coupla more cowpokes if we're goin' callin' on the Diamond-8 in the mornin'."

"I don't reckon so," from Jugandel. "You see, there's just the three Du Sangs left there, now—and two of them is crippled."

"Sure enough," Norris responded. "I'd forgot about the crew pullin' freight."

Jugandel left to go to the bunkhouse after a time. Jerry finished with the dishes, and she and Melody went out to sit in front of the house. They confessed a desire to watch the moon rise, but Tom Norris didn't wholly believe them. As he himself said, "Bein' as I ain't interested none in

145

astronomy an' such, I reckon I'll turn in. Goin' to try and hairpin a bronc in the mornin', so I can make that ride to the Diamond-8 with you boys. Right now I'm bettin' a stack of blues that two moons could rise, and you younkers wouldn't see either of 'em, half the time!"

Which, after all, was more or less true.

The bunkhouse was dark by the time Jerry and Melody arose from their seats on the ranch house porch. Melody entered the house a minute to get his guns which he had left in the kitchen, then reluctantly said good-night to the girl and bent his steps toward the bunkhouse.

When nearly to the building, he swung over toward the corral. Taking his rig from the top bar where he had left it, he entered the enclosure and proceeded to saddle Jezebel. Then he led the mare out, and left her standing a short distance from the bunkhouse.

Now he was forced to proceed with more caution. He entered the bunkhouse, listened carefully, and detected five distinct snores. All of the men were asleep, including Jugandel. Melody scratched a match and looked quickly about the room. One of the sleepers stirred uneasily. The match was quickly extinguished, but Melody had seen what he was searching for. Moving on tiptoe across the room, he picked from a table the skinned-out roll of cowhide bearing the blotted Rafter-S brand and silently vanished through the door.

Five minutes later Jezebel was carrying him with swift ground-covering strides, across the range toward the Diamond-8.

## 22.
## *Melody Corners the Du Sangs*

IT WAS well past midnight when Melody splashed across the shallow Latigo River, and turned the little mare on a course that bore slightly to the southwest. It would be a matter of another six or seven miles before he reached the Du Sang ranch.

The earth unrolled swiftly beneath Jezebel's flying hoofs. Once, Melody drew out his guns, one after the other, and examined them with a grunt of satisfaction. Then he replaced them in holsters.

Finally, topping a rise of ground, he glimpsed some distance down the slope the blocky outlines of the Diamond-8 adobe buildings. On a lower floor of the two-story ranch house a lamp shone from one window. Melody checked the mare to a walk and proceeded more slowly. When nearly to the house, he guided Jezebel toward a small clump of cotton-woods. Here he dismounted and tossing the reins over a lower branch, finished the journey on foot.

Arriving before the house, he paused a moment to slip off his boots, then in sock feet, made his way up to the building and noiselessly entered by the front door which happened to be unlocked. Like a shadow the cowboy flitted inside, and found himself in a large room, which was dark. Across the room was a second doorway through which came light and voices.

Moving with cat-like tread, Melody slipped softly across the floor and took up a stand to one side of the doorway. Guy and Hugo Du Sang were talking.

"—and you got some scheme brewin'," Hugo was saying. "I saw you talking to the men before they left. It's all right for you to say that you thought you'd give them a chance to get a drink, but I figure there's more to it than that."

"All right, I'll tell you," Guy said. "Mebbe you'll be

sore, and mebbe you won't, but I give the men certain orders, and told them they come from you."

"You gotta heap of nerve," Hugo growled. "What was them orders?"

Guy explained. "I told the boys to ride into Vaca Wells and spread the news that they'd had an argument with us and was quittin'. They'll hang around town for a spell, then pull out—all of 'em ridin' east, like they was gettin' out of the country——"

"A hell of an order to give, when we may be needin' a full force at any time," Hugo rasped.

"Wait a minute. Once outta sight of Vaca Wells, they'll swing wide and come back here. They oughta be comin' pretty soon."

"You don't know that gang like I do," Hugo laughed scornfully. "They'll probably all get drunk and come back when they feel like it."

"They'll be back before mornin', anyhow. Tomorrow afternoon they can lay out in the brush, back of the Rafter-S, and pick off Madigan and his men when they come ridin' in at night. That outfit is combin' the hills for stock, and they never come in in a bunch. The boys'll be able to ambush 'em one at a time. It might be a good idea to kill off Norris first, while he's alone——"

"Well, you damn fool!" came Hugo's angry voice. "What's the idea of startin' a game like this without me knowin' it?"

"I figured you might buck the scheme," Guy said bitterly, "but dammit, Hugo, this outfit is as much mine as yours. It's time I had a say in the runnin' of it. Your ideas ain't worked worth a hoot in hell, and that Madigan hombre has got things pretty much his own way. It's our last chance, unless you got somethin' better to offer. The boys will see you, before they head for the Rafter-S, so if you don't want 'em to go, you can stop 'em. If you got a better idea, say so."

"I ain't," Hugo growled admission, "but I ain't stuck on yours, neither."

"Well, we gotta have some action purty quick," Guy said sullenly.

For a few moments the talk wasn't resumed. Melody heard the clink of glasses against a bottle, then a smacking of lips. He edged forward and peered cautiously around the doorway.

It was a room of considerable size with, at the opposite side, a second doorway that opened to the back of the house. To the right was a flight of wooden stairs that led to the upper floor, and at the other side of the room was a cot upon which lay Luke Du Sang, covered with blankets. The upper part of Luke's body was swathed in bandages and he appeared to be asleep.

At a table in the center of the room sat Guy and Hugo, with a bottle of whisky between them. Hugo's back was to Melody, while Guy sat farther around to the side. Neither could see the doorway, where Melody stood, without turning in their chairs. Guy's arm was still in a sling. A belt and gun hung on a wooden peg driven into one of the adobe walls. Probably, Guy's weapon, or Luke's. Guy was unarmed at the moment, although Hugo wore his brace of ivory-butted forty-fives.

Guy again took up the conversation. "It looks like the best bet to me. We can wipe out the Rafter-S all at once——"

"That's just what I don't like about your idea," Hugo cut in. "Everybody knows that me and Norris has had trouble. If the Rafter-S got wiped out, suspicion would sure as hell point my way. And there's the gal, too——"

"Let suspicion point from here to Hades!" Guy snapped. "What do you care? Suspicion ain't proof." He moved his unbandaged hand to the bottle and poured another drink. "You're gettin' awful skeery all of a sudden, Hugo. Doc Kenyon will be here tomorrow afternoon to see Luke. We'll manage to keep him here the rest of the day. That'll make an alibi for you'n me, see?"

Hugo shook his head dubiously. "It'll sure raise a heap of hell."

By now Melody had shifted the roll of skinned-out brand under one arm, and moved into the doorway. Neither of the Du Sangs heard him, as he stood leaning nonchalantly against the door jamb. The cowboy hadn't drawn his guns, but his hands hovered close to holsters.

Guy was laughing nastily now. "Who do you figure will raise any hell, Hugo? With Higley gone, there ain't no law officer to take the matter up. By the time they'd get one down here, things will have blown over. Our men can drift back here one at a time, when everything has quieted down. It might be a good idea to bury all of the bodies, before anybody gets wind of what's happened. It'll just be

149

a mysterious disappearance. I can't see why the idea don't appeal to you, so long as nobody can't hang anythin' on us."

"But the gal——" Hugo commenced.

"Hang the girl!" Guy exclaimed impatiently. "If you're afeared to rub her out—why, we'll get rid of her some other way. Now, make up your mind. The boys will be back pretty soon. Are you goin' to send 'em to the Rafter-S, or are you goin' to lay down and lose your nerve? Either the Rafter-S goes down, or we do! Which is it to be?"

Hugo threw both hands into the air with a gesture of consent. "All right," he said hopelessly, "you win. Tell the boys I said to go ahead, when they come back. We simply gotta have the Rafter-S——"

"Try and get it!" Melody spoke suddenly. He had been unable to contain himself any longer. "Not a move, Du Sang!" he added swiftly. "I'll be pluggin' you, first chance!"

Hugo Du Sang abruptly went rigid in his chair, back still turned to Melody. Guy Du Sang had started to rise, but now sank back with a curse. Still, Melody had made no move to draw his guns.

Hugo recognized the cowboy's voice. "You damn' redhead!" he spat venomously. "What you doin' here?"

"Take a chance, Hugo, take a chance," Guy urged. "He ain't got his guns out——"

"Neither have you, feller," Melody laughed softly. "I can fill my hand and roll lead a heap faster than either of you, so just take it easy."

Guy glanced longingly at the gun hanging on the wall, but didn't dare try to reach it. "Well, what's the game?" he snarled.

The loud voices had aroused the sleeping Luke. He opened his eyes, recognized Melody, cursed weakly, but seemed unable to do more.

"Now that you fellers are calmed down," Melody continued after a moment, "I'll give you the reasons for my visit. In the first place, I wa'n't fooled a bit by the news that your crew had quit. I knew they was some plan afoot, so I thought I'd drift over and see could I learn what it was. I did—and it's a pretty lousy game!"

He paused a moment, then tossed the skinned-out portion of hide over Hugo's head, to land on the table. "Give a look at that, you thievin' coyotes," he went on. "Several others have seen it, beside myself, so it don't matter much, if I don't get it back. We could pro'bly get some more of the same evidence, if it was needed."

There was nothing else to do. Hugo Du Sang unrolled the piece of green hide, then suddenly burst into a fit of cursing in which he was joined by Guy. Both knew that denial was useless.

Hugo tried to bluff it out. "Well, what about it?" he growled.

"Just this." Melody's tones were sharp. "I've been checking over the Rafter-S tally book, Du Sang, and I figure if it hadn't been for you rustlin' hombres, Norris could have paid off his mortgage by this time."

"What about it?" Hugo repeated.

"Du Sang," Melody explained, "I ain't forgot that you acted sorta square that day I come over here and killed Manitoba. I'm tryin' to even that account, and give you a chance to get out with a whole skin. We got plenty evidence against you, if we take this matter to court. But courts take pretty long to get goin' sometimes. You're holdin' that Rafter-S mortgage paper. I want it, in exchange for that brand-blottin' evidence. After that, you fellers can leave the country and nothin' more will be said."

"You can go to hell, that's what you can do," Guy sneered.

"Don't let him get away with that," Luke croaked from his cot.

Hugo was more calm. "You want that mortgage for this piece of hide, eh? Madigan, that ain't accordin' to law. If you think you got anythin' on us, you better take the matter to court." He was stalling for time, hoping for the arrival of the Diamond-8 punchers. Hugo shifted slightly in his chair as he spoke the words.

"None of that, Du Sang!" Melody ordered swiftly. "I want your back to me. Don't try to turn around." Again, Hugo settled in his chair.

Melody continued the conversation, "I've just told you that I'd just as soon this matter didn't get into the courts. Hell! I don't want that mortgage tied up in no law courts. It might take a long time to get things unraveled. I got another reason for takin' this action. We could come over and put on a big fight, and probably clean you out, but I don't see no reason for sheddin' blood if it can be avoided. Gimme that mortgage. That's all I'm askin', but you've got to make up your mind pronto!"

"I ain't got that paper," Hugo lied.

"I don't bluff easy," Melody snapped tartly. "Du Sang, you're just the sort of hombre that would keep a paper of that sort close to you. Now, c'mon, lemme have it."

Du Sang stirred uneasily. "S'posin' I don't see it your way?"

"You will," Melody laughed coolly, "or I'm li'ble to get impatient and start rollin' my lead."

Du Sang didn't reply at once. He had sensed something grim in that laugh. Melody could feel the eyes of the wounded Luke on him. He hoped that Luke didn't have a gun concealed beneath his blankets. Guy was cursing in a savage undertone, his eyes a poisonous glare of hate.

"All right," Hugo finally consented. "I'll get it." He started to rise from his chair.

"Sit right where you are, Du Sang!" Melody barked. Du Sang sank back. "I ain't trustin' you, Du Sang," the cowboy continued. "Tell your brother to get it for me."

A look of disappointment, which Melody couldn't see, passed across Hugo's features. Hugo looked at his brother, then nodded to Guy. "Go get it," he said. Guy got to his feet.

"I'm hopin'," Melody drawled, "that the paper is in this room. Otherwise, Du Sang, I'll have to have your brother tie you up, while I go along with him to get that mortgage—and if they's any tyin' up to be done, I'll give the knots a plumb thorough examination before I leave you alone. I don't trust you hombres—none a-tall!"

Guy's face clouded up like a thunderstorm. He stood at the table, uncertain how to proceed. Hugo couldn't quite suppress the chuckle of admiration that passed his lips. "You got a good head on you, Madigan," he conceded grudgingly. "All right, you win. The mortgage is in a drawer in this table. I can reach it, myself."

"Just make sure you don't pull no hawg-laigs outta that drawer," Melody warned coldly. "And don't make no fast moves or I'm li'ble to think you're tryin' somethin'."

Mentally, Hugo cursed the awkward position in which Melody had found him. Due to the arms on the chair in which he was seated, it was impossible for Hugo to make a quick draw without rising. Even then, he'd have to turn to face Melody.

152

Guy was still standing by the table. Hugo bent forward slowly, pulled open the drawer beneath the table's leaf, and after a moment drew out several papers. He sorted them over, finally selected one in a long envelope, and passed it to Guy. "Hand that to Madigan," he ordered. A look of understanding passed between the two men in that instant. Hugo was staking everything he had on one play.

Melody watched the two warily as Guy crossed the room, the envelope in one outstretched hand. The very ease with which Du Sang had surrendered the paper, made Melody suspicious. He felt there was something in the air, but couldn't decide just what it was. Hugo sat as before; Guy was unarmed; Luke was stretched helpless, in bed.

Melody accepted the envelope from Guy's hand, then, "Back where you were, feller," he ordered. "I don't want to shoot an unarmed man, but at the same time I ain't trustin' you. I'll draw if you force me to." He glanced quickly at the envelope in his hand, then spoke to Hugo, as Guy retreated to the table. "How am I to know this is the mortgage paper?" he asked.

And that was exactly what Hugo had been waiting for. "You'll have to take my word for it," he replied carelessly, "or else look at the paper. That envelope ain't sealed."

# PART VI

# The Fight at the Diamond-8

## 23.

MELODY didn't miss the challenge in the words. "Oh, yeah," he answered, "I might do that. I don't know much about readin' mortgages, though."

He was watching Du Sang closely now. The cowboy could see that Hugo was alert for the first rustle of paper. Melody laughed softly, and drew one thumb-nail across the envelope. It sounded exactly as though the paper were being drawn out.

There was no time for Guy to warn his brother of the trick. Like a flash Hugo left his chair and whirled, hands reaching to holsters. A savage curse parted his lips, as he found himself looking directly into Melody's guns!

At the first movement, Melody had dropped the envelope and drawn his own forty-fives. It was all one smooth, eye-defying operation—the drawing of guns, the swift lift of barrels, the thumbing of savage explosions!

Du Sang's six shooters flamed at almost the same instant, but both shots missed. Melody had leaped sideways, into the room, even as he unleashed his lead. He fired again, as Hugo swung his heavy guns in swift arcs that covered the moving cowboy. Hugo's big body was lifted and thrown as though struck by some tremendous invisible force, but his aim wasn't completely spoiled.

Something struck Melody's shoulder a terrific impact, whirled him half off balance, sent him staggering back against the edge of the doorway. At the same instant, a leaden slug ripped into his leg, and finished the upsetting process! The cowboy suddenly found himself sprawled on the floor! Luckily, he had retained the hold on his guns.

But Hugo Du Sang was done for. Through a swirl of gray, Melody saw the big man go crashing across the room to fall on the floor beside Luke's cot. Melody's eyes shifted to Luke, now sitting upright, struggling to reach one of Hugo's guns. Melody raised one gun to stop the move, then suddenly thought of Guy.

The cowboy twisted around, just as Guy overturned the table. It fell with a crash and shattering of glass as the lamp went to the floor and was instantly extinguished. Melody fired by instinct, heard Guy's yelp of pain, then stumbling footsteps. Guy was trying to reach that gun hanging on the wall.

The room was in Stygian darkness, now. Gritting his teeth against the pain, Melody crawled to another position. At the same moment a vicious stab of crimson ripped the gloom. A second later, there came a second shot from the vicinity of the cot. Both Guy and Luke were armed, now.

Again Melody shifted position. Neither of the shots had struck him, but they had come dangerously close. He propped himself in a sitting posture, back braced against the wall near the doorway. There was an instant's silence. Melody felt himself growing weak. He decided to finish things before the Diamond-8 men arrived.

Laughing grimly, the cowboy thumbed one swift shot at the point where he guessed Guy to be standing. Again, he was rewarded by a sharp yelp of pain.

Then hell broke loose! The room was illuminated by the brilliant flashes of light from the Du Sang guns! The house rocked with the concussions of the heavy weapons. Leaden messengers of death buzzed like angry hornets, and thudded into the wall at the cowboy's back, as the hammers slipped rapidly under his thumbs!

He heard a body strike the floor, knew that Guy Du Sang was finished. At the same instant another slug ripped into Melody's body. He was feeling deathly sick, now. It was all a crimson blur of smoke and roaring guns. The world reeled madly. Burnt powder stung eyes and throat and nostrils. Still, the cowboy fought grimly on. He realized quite suddenly that his hammers had been falling on empty shells for some time. He ceased working them. The room had gone strangely quiet.

"C'mon, you snakes," he called defiance, "let's finish it!"

His voice was a harsh croak, now, and he was too far gone to realize there had been no answering shot to his challenge. Somehow, he managed to extract the empty shells from his cylinders. "Stallin', that's what they're doin'," he mumbled thickly. "I'll show 'em what six-guns is really for."

For a few brief moments his fingers fumbled at cartridges in his belts, then everything went black and he toppled to one side.

Dawn was creeping in at the windows before Melody regained consciousness. He was stretched on the cot but lately occupied by Luke Du Sang. Things came back to him slowly, before he noticed an anxious group of worried faces bent above him. Gradually, he picked out the features of the Rafter-S crew. Events commenced to shape themselves more clearly, after that.

"Woke up, eh?" It was Jugandel's voice.

Melody nodded weakly and tried to rise. A hundred twinges of pain sent him to a reclining position, again. "Am I hit bad?" he muttered.

"Not bad, but often." It was Tom Norris speaking, now. "You'll be fit as a fiddle in a few weeks, son. But of all the damn' fool plays to make. We found that mortgage on the floor——"

"Keep it. That's what I come for." Melody smiled feebly. "Did I get Du Sang?"

"Get him?" Mesquite Farrell snorted. "Cowboy, you got three Du Sangs! Hugo lived long enough after we got here to confess everythin' he'd planned and the things he'd already done—stealin' stock from the other spreads, and so on. Guy and Luke is still livin', and may pull through to face a long jail sentence."

"But—but I don't understand," Melody frowned. "How'd you fellers happen to come here?"

"Jug-Handle woke up and heard you ridin' away," Norris explained. "He figured that was sorta funny so he got up and discovered that skinned-out piece of hide was missin'. Right away he guessed you'd come here. He got the rest of us up and into saddles before we knew what it was all about—even me what ain't hairpinned a bronc in months."

Jugandel took up the story. "We was nearly here when we heard the shots. Then the light went out and there was a heap more shootin'. It had all died down, though, before we come in the house. We could hear you mumblin' somethin' about finishin' the fight, so we busted right in. Lord! When we found a lamp and lit it, this room looked like a tornado had swept through. While Norris was tendin' to

157

you, I was questionin' Hugo Du Sang before he died. It was Manitoba that murdered our other Association detective. Du Sang confessed everythin'——"

"About intendin' to send his crew over to ambush us?" Melody queried.

"Yeah, that, too," Jugandel nodded. "So we was waitin' for them Diamond-8 snakes when they rode in from town. We'd already found the Chino cook, scared to death, almost, in the cook shanty. Anyway, we laid low when them Diamond-8 punchers arrived. They was all drunker than hoot-owls, and headed direct for the bunkhouse. Then we dropped down and made 'em prisoners. Easiest thing you ever saw. Now, that we got 'em all tied up, they're plumb eager to turn state's evidence to save their own skins. They'll tell everythin' they know. Cowboy, this neck of the range is cleaned up proper, and there's a heap of thanks owin' to you——"

"You ain't so bad yourself," Melody grunted. "In fact, all you fellers has done as much as me——" A cry of protest went up which he interrupted with, "Was Jerry all right when you left?"

"Hell, son," Norris replied, "do you think Jerry would be left behind at a time like this? She come, too, totin' her gun an' ready for trouble. She's upstairs, now, lookin' for some cloths to use for bandages. Who do you think fixed you up like this?"

For the first time Melody noticed the bandages on his body.

"Matt Oliver has gone to Vaca Wells for Doc Kenyon," Norris continued. He checked himself suddenly and looked somewhat concerned. "That reminds me, Jerry said you wa'n't to be bothered or talked to, if you woke up. She'll give us hell for goin' against her orders."

Melody's ears caught a light, quick footstep, then, "Melody!" Jerry cried.

Somehow the men faded out of the room, after that. Melody saw Jerry's face nearing his own, felt warm arms encircling him. Maybe he passed out from sheer happiness. Perhaps, unbelievable as it way seem under the circumstances, he just went to sleep. Anyway, the sun was shining into the room when he again opened his eyes. Jerry was seated next to his cot. The cowboy was feeling stronger already.

The girl caught the sound of his voice and turned. There

were the usual preliminaries to be indulged in, before he spoke again. Then, "It's sure goin' to be great," he told her.

"What is?"

"Havin' you around always, and things peaceful and all, like they're bound to be. I'll have to get out my accordion, and play you a song I been makin' up lately."

"What's it about, cowboy?"

Melody's eyes widened. "My gosh, girl, don't you know? . . . Why, it's 'bout you'n me, of course! Nothin' else matters, does it?"

And from the manner of her answer, it may be judged that nothing else did matter, at least to Jerry and Melody Madigan.

# GREAT WESTERN ADVENTURE
## FROM ◆ AVON

| | | |
|---|---|---|
| **ACTION AT ARCANUM** | | |
| William Colt MacDonald | 14332 | .75 |
| **APPLEGATE'S GOLD** | | |
| Todhunter Ballard | 17525 | .75 |
| **CAT EYES** | | |
| Richard Brister | 15065 | .75 |
| **GUN SHY** | | |
| Mitchell Dana | 14779 | .75 |
| **HIGH IRON** | | |
| Todhunter Ballard | 01438 | .60 |
| **THE KANSAN** | | |
| Richard Brister | 15917 | .75 |
| **THE LAST BUFFALO** | | |
| Mitchell Dana | 14522 | .75 |
| **LAW KILLER** | | |
| Richard Brister | 16790 | .75 |
| **LEAD RECKONING** | | |
| Ray Hogan | 18065 | .75 |
| **THE MOONLIGHTERS** | | |
| Ray Hogan | 18879 | .75 |
| **NIGHT RAIDER** | | |
| Ray Hogan | 18549 | .75 |
| **PLUNDER CANYON** | | |
| Todhunter Ballard | 17673 | .75 |
| **RENEGADE BRAND** | | |
| Richard Brister | 17152 | .75 |
| **SHOOTOUT AT SENTINEL PEAK** | | |
| Richard Brister | 16519 | .75 |
| **STIR UP THE DUST** | | |
| William Colt MacDonald | 04697 | .75 |
| **TOWN WITHOUT A PRAYER** | | |
| Mitchell Dana | 04457 | .75 |
| **WOLF STREAK** | | |
| Richard Brister | 15321 | .75 |

---